The Sneaker Tree

Phil Taylor

If you're reading this story on an e-reader or an IPad with a Wi-Fi connection, feel free to click on the words highlighted in blue. They are live links to related and possibly entertaining material.

Edited by Cynthia Shepp
www.cynthiashepp.com

The inspiration for the title and inclusion of The Sneaker Tree in the story came from The Sneaker Trees of Lyndonville, NY. There are however trees full of shoes all over the United States and the world and each has its own unique story. To read more about them go to:
http://www.roadsideamerica.com/story/29064

Chapter 1

This day was perfect. A crisp, azure sky as far as the eye could see with only a few pristine white, puffy clouds daring to interrupt its glorious expanse. The air was still and warm. It was the first day that didn't have even a hint of dampness or chill in the air. The trees seemed to be bursting with a deep, rich green, as their splendidly attired branches appeared to reach for that incredibly perfect sky. I had never seen anyone die, and the magnificent afternoon gave no hint of what was to come.

We had talked during the day at school. As we did on almost every sunny, spring afternoon, we hopped off the bus and literally sprinted to our houses to get our gear.

Some days I just dropped my backpack on the porch, gave a shout to my mom, grabbed my glove and bat, and ran to meet the guys at the field behind the elementary school at the end of our street.

Some days we had enough guys for a good six-on-six game and on other days, if we were short, we'd have to use ghost runners and phantom fielders. The neighborhood baseball field was our *Field of Dreams*. In a day and age when most of our classmates headed for the couch and their video games, our little group of friends was a throwback to an earlier time. We still enjoyed nothing more than hearing the crack of the bat, or, since we mostly had aluminum bats, the ping of the bat. We all loved baseball, and we all imagined we'd be playing in the big leagues someday. Baseball would indeed turn out to be my salvation that summer, but not in the way I imagined.

As usual, I got there first. The sun washed over the field as if cleansing it just for us. I hesitated for a moment before crossing the white line, before stepping onto the field. To me, a perfectly mown field with fresh lines and a sky full of sunshine looked like a cathedral. Because of its beauty, I was hesitant to break the silence, to soil the sacred ground with my footsteps. To me, even then, baseball was one of the few things that were unspoiled by technology or changed by time. To me, baseball was something pure that filled me with a joy nothing else did. I just stood there for a moment, gazing at the mound, the base paths, and home plate.

Then there was a *whoosh* of air as something brushed my head as it flew by. "Hey stupid, are you asleep over there?" He threw his mitt, just barely missing my head. It was Gooby. He was my best friend, but he didn't share my passion, my worship of baseball. To him, a field was just a field. As Gooby arrived, I could see Cliff, Chuck, Bolo, and Scooter all coming down the street and across the field at various rates of enthusiasm. Before long, a couple of the guys from the street over arrived and we had enough to get a game going. We'd add people as they showed up if need be, even if we ended up with too many.

We spent a few minutes screwing around, complaining about homework, talking about girls we liked, and discussing who was on our Little League teams this year. We were all around twelve and this was to be our last year of Little League. This was the year that making the league All-Star team might even mean a trip to the Little League World Series, if we could keep winning. Although we were dreaming of being on TV in the Little League World Series, we still saw baseball as nothing but pure, unadulterated fun. We played with our friends and someone's dad was the coach. We got to wear uniforms that were t-shirts with a major-league logo on the front and a car dealer-sponsorship logo on the back. Every game, win or lose, was still followed by a snack someone's parent had brought. This was going to be our last year to just enjoy baseball for what it was—just a game. Next year, we would be playing on the big fields for school and travel teams that took winning seriously and some of us might not make that cut.

This year was going to be really fun for some of us. We were starting to hit puberty and getting a little bigger and stronger. I had never hit a home run, at least one that left the park. Last year, I came close once. I did hit two inside-the-park homers that were due as much to the other teams inept fielding as any skills I might possess. This year though, I wanted to hit one out. Just one. I had seen a couple of the other, bigger kids do it last year, and I wanted that. I wanted to be the one watching the ball land on the other side of the fence and hearing the cheers as I circled the bases to run into my teammates gathering at home plate to pat me on the back. *This year is going to be my year,* I told myself.

Once we chose teams, Scooter took the mound and

immediately started in. *"Bases loaded with Red Sox. Full count. Righetti leans in to receive the sign from Cerone. He gets his signature pitch, a tailing fastball high in the strike zone. Righetti is one pitch away from sending the Yankees to the World Series to face the New York Mets. He winds up. The pitch to Boggs...."*

Scooter was our unofficial play-by-play guy, even when he was playing, including running the bases. Typically, his mouth ran faster than he did, and when we played, it was always Yankees versus Red Sox. Despite the fact that Scooter's dad had nicknamed him after the famous Yankees shortstop, Phil Rizzuto, Scooter had always wanted to be a pitcher. His dad was an old time Yankees fan and liked Phil Rizzuto because he was Italian like his family was. Scooter was a Righetti fan, which was still ok with his dad, but the nickname Scooter had been attached to him from birth.

Out of us all, Nathan "Scooter" Grottanelli was

probably the best baseball player. He practiced year round, even, much to his parents chagrin, swinging a baseball bat in his room in front of the mirror hundreds of times a day so he could watch his form. He was so good that he never, not even once, broke anything swinging a bat in the house. He couldn't make the same claim in regards to practicing his pitching in the house, but he was still pretty good.

Scooter even practiced baseball unconsciously just about anywhere he was. If we were just walking around the block talking or just hanging out playing cards, without thinking about it, he often mimed a throwing motion repeatedly. Even when he played the field, in between the action, he would practice his swing with an imaginary bat.

His room was the best too. His dad had painted the bottom half of the walls blue to match the outfield wall at Yankee Stadium, including stenciling in the distance in each corner and where centerfield would be if his room were the stadium. The top half of the walls were white with blue pinstripes, just like the Yankees home uniforms, and covered in Yankees pictures and paraphernalia.

TING! I'd love to romanticize it and say "CRACK" as if it were a wooden bat, but it wasn't. It was one of those shiny aluminum ones, where the barrel had that trampoline effect so that one-hundred-pound kids like us could feel like big shots hitting it out of a 210-foot Little League park. Chuck had gotten a serious piece of this one, and it was headed back where it came from in a hurry. Then we all did hear a loud crack. It was a sickening, horrifying crack. It was the ball hitting Scooter in the chest. It happened so fast that he didn't have a chance to get his glove up in front of the line drive as it rocketed off the bat. Chuck didn't even start to run to first base. He and I reached Scooter at the same time. The ball had hit him square in the chest, and Scooter had hit the ground like someone had dropped a bag of sand.

I can still remember it, and in my head, it always

seems to happen in slow motion. I can still picture myself running towards him, but in my recollection, I still never get there in time. From my position at first base, I watched as the ball sped in a perfectly straight-line right back, almost to the exact point where Scooter had released it. Only when it got there, Scooter was just standing up from his follow through, and it hit him directly in the center of his sternum. I was closest to him and heard the crack as the bone in his chest gave a little. His eyes got big for a fraction of a second and then went blank, as his knees suddenly seemed to forget their responsibility for holding him upright. His arms dropped to his sides as he dropped to his knees on the mound and then fell to his side. The ball had hit the ground in front of him and rolled to the front of the mound.

In my nightmares, as well as in real life, it wouldn't matter how quickly I ran. Scooter was dead before he hit the ground. Although I was only twelve, I tried to give him mouth to mouth and CPR like I had seen on television, while Gooby ran home to tell his mom to call for an ambulance. I can still remember the salty taste of his sweat on my lips as I attempted to resuscitate him. Since then, whenever I taste my own sweat on a hot, summer day, the memory of Scooter's dead lips against mine turns my stomach and knocks the wind out of me.

I knew it was bad because, unless I was blowing into his mouth, his chest wasn't rising and falling as we waited there for the ambulance. The wait was probably only a few minutes, but it seemed like forever. The other guys were gathered in a loose circle around the mound as I knelt in the dirt, trying to breathe every bit of life I had into Scooter. The only sound other than my inhalation and exhalation was the song of the late afternoon crickets until finally, mercifully, the wail of a siren grew near.

The circle parted as the EMTs dragged a gurney across the field. "It's okay kid. I'll take over now," said one of the EMTs as she gently stepped next to me and placed one of those pump-bag-type gadgets over Scooter's mouth. She continued pumping air into his lungs as they wheeled him away. Within minutes, Scooter, the EMT's and all the adults that had rushed to the field were gone as quickly as they had arrived, leaving us in a stunned silence. The day was still sunny and beautiful, and the late afternoon crickets had resumed their song as if nothing had happened.

Chapter 2

I had only been to one funeral before. It was for my grandfather, who had passed away after a long illness, and all the adults had agreed that it was a blessing. I was eight at the time and could never understand how losing someone you loved could ever be a blessing. Then, as now, I'm pretty sure death is always bad. I don't ever want to lose anyone I love and then, as now, I'm pretty sure that if I have the choice to be alive versus dead, I'm picking alive every time.

Grampa's funeral had been a very sedate affair with, much to my horror, an open casket. I wasn't sure it was even him in there. He looked plastic, fake, kind of like a mannequin of my grandfather. They consoled my gramma, telling her that he was in a better place and looking down on her.

They told lots of old stories, some of which were even a little funny. I loved my grampa, but now I was stuck forever with that last image of him. I didn't want a last image like that of Scooter.

When I walked in, I could see with some relief that the casket was closed. It was smaller than my grampa's, which made it seem even sadder, and it had a big, blown-up picture of Scooter from Little League on it and, right next to it, his baseball glove. It was the gray and black Nike model that he was so proud of. I had been so jealous of that glove when he got it, but now I couldn't stand to see it there. It was right though, that he should be buried with it. If there was a heaven, I'm sure Scooter would be playing ball there. Thank God, Scooter's wasn't an open-casket affair. I don't think I could have handled that. Not seeing Scooter all dead and made up somehow. In my mind, it made it seem like maybe he wasn't really dead.

When the priest and some of Scooter's relatives got up to talk, I didn't really listen. I didn't want to. I didn't want to hear about or think about Scooter being dead. I knew some funny stories about Scooter, but I doubted the adults would let me get up and talk. It didn't matter anyway. The adults sat up front and made Goob, Cliff, Chuck, Bolo, me, and the other "kids", sit in the back row, as if our sadness wasn't as important as theirs was. I didn't think they'd let me tell the story about Scooter farting out loud during the math test anyway. It was funny though, especially when Gooby got blamed for it, but it wasn't the kind of funny that adults liked, so I just stayed quiet mostly. I had wanted all of us to come in our Little League uniforms because I know that Scooter would like that, but the adults told us it was a funeral, and we had to wear ties and stuff.

"Lookit that," Chuck said in a pressured whisper. "They got his Cubs picture from last year. How could they do that? Everybody knows he likes the Yankees. His friggin' nickname is Scooter!" A couple of adults turned and gave us the evil eye.

I leaned over to Chuck. With my lips almost touching his ear, I whispered, "They haven't given out this year's pictures yet. We get 'em next week."

I looked up and saw Scooter's mom at the end of the front row, leaning into his dad and just sobbing uncontrollably. Her breath was short and clipped, and her shoulders shuddered with each fresh sob. Then it really hit me. Scooter's parents would never be getting a Little

League picture again. Then a tear slipped from my eye as I realized that somewhere, there were pictures of Scooter, taken just two weeks ago, in his uniform for this year's team. Would his parents still get them? What would they do with them? Could I ask for one to keep in my sock for good luck?

Scooter was never playing Little League again. Not with me or anyone else. He wasn't home sick with the flu or on vacation. He was up front in that glossy, mahogany box with his picture and glove on top. That was Scooter now. I could feel the lump in my throat growing, and I had to get up and get out of there. I could feel the tears welling up in my eyes and if I didn't get out, I was going to be just like Scooter's mom in a minute.

Chapter 3

When I got home, it started again. The fighting. I had no idea what it was about this time, and I didn't care. After a while, it had just become background noise to me. It was the soundtrack to my life. *Jesus Christ*, I thought to myself as I lay on my bed. *What the fuck is wrong with them?* I swore like that all the time, but only in my head. Well, that's not true. Sometimes when I was stuck playing the outfield, I'd practice my swearing out loud, because I knew no one could hear me.

We had just come from my friends' funeral and as usual, they were bickering about something that would be long forgotten by the time they started their next fight about something else tomorrow. *Did they care?* I wondered. *Did they care that Scooter was dead?* It sure didn't seem like it. I wonder if they'd just go right back to fighting if it was my funeral that had just ended. I couldn't believe how selfish they were. Scooter was like a brother to me.

Scooter had slept over at my house countless times.

We swam in each other's pools all summer long, and he had even gone camping with my family for a week once. Scooter and the other guys were part of my family. We all grew up in the same neighborhood, and it was the best neighborhood in the world as far as we were concerned. We felt like we were the kings of it.

I think I spent more time with Scooter, Gooby, Cliff, Bolo, and Chuck than I did with my own parents. In fact, during the summer, when we were out of school and all our parents were working, we pretty much took care of ourselves all day, every day. We would pass the time, day after day, walking around the neighborhood or hanging out at whoevers house we settled at to play Nintendo or watch television. When we were lucky, we would go out to the woods and blow up action figures with fireworks that Ronnie from down the street had gotten for us when his cousin had driven to Pennsylvania. We were brothers. At least it felt that way, and I needed brothers that summer more than ever.

The guys. That was what I called them when my mom asked where I was going, or who I was going to be with. Scooter, Gooby, Cliff, Bolo, and Chuck. They were *the guys*. It wasn't always all of us together, but often it was. We had a bond. We didn't call it that or talk about it, but it was there nonetheless. We had all known each other since we could remember. We weren't all the same age, but we were close enough that it didn't matter.

Chuck, being about two years younger than we were, often got the little-brother treatment from the rest of us. His name wasn't really Chuck either. That was a nickname Bolo's older brother, Scott, had bestowed upon him. Chuck's real name was Brian, but one day without provocation, Scott had decided that Brian looked like someone named "Chuckie Huddleburger". I have no idea why, but we thought that was hilarious. After a summer of calling him Chuck, it just became his name to us. I can't even imagine calling him anything else. We heaped a fair amount of teasing and abuse on Chuck because he was younger, but he hung around with us anyway, accepting the teasing as the price he had to pay to be part of our little cohort. As much as we picked on him, we would have fought anyone else that tried to treat him the same way. Chuck did have brothers, but I like to think that by virtue of the time we spent together, the rest of us were more brothers to him than they were.

Gooby was a nickname too, of course. That started when we were all about ten years old. At the end of our street was a police station. Each winter the snow plows would create huge mountains of snow on the edges of the parking lot when they cleared it. In the winter Gooby, Cliff, Chuck, Bolo, Scooter, and I would bundle ourselves up in our snow clothes and head down to the police station. The police had gotten to know us from our frequent trips into the lobby to get drinks of water and pick up the cool bumper stickers they gave out. When we got to the snowy police station parking lot, we would play a reverse *King of the Hill* kind of game. We'd climb to the top of one of those towering piles of snow and one of us would expectorate a big, green goober upon the top of the hill. Then, as soon as someone said, "GO!" we would battle to push each other onto the top of the mountain.

Gooby, as a ten year old, had the physical build of a newborn deer, all spindly bones and no muscle mass whatsoever. Needless to say, he lost our pre-pubescent manhood contest more often than not, and ended up with a frozen goober stuck to his parka, and so a nickname was born. It was harmless enough, but Goob's dad was never too fond of the nickname. Gooby was the most intellectual of us. He was kind of our groups Cliff Clavin. He always had an obscure fact about something. We'd be walking along and a plane would fly overhead, and he'd say something like, "That's a Cessna 780 Twin Turbo Prop

Crop Duster," or some such nonsense. We never knew if he was right, or if he was making stuff up.

Bolo was also a nickname. I know this is starting to sound redundant. It wasn't a concerted effort on our part to hand out nicknames, they just sort of happened. Bolo's name was actually Robert Ruttinger. We didn't actually give him the nickname. My mom did, kind of accidentally. When we were younger, we called him Bob. One day I arrived home after school, and my mom wasn't home yet. I planned to go hang out with Bob after school, so I left a note that said, "I'm at Bob's house". Unfortunately, in my hurried handwriting, to my mother, the word "Bob" looked like "Bolo." So she spent the afternoon calling neighbors in a panic because she didn't know who 'Bolo' was, and why he had taken her son. Needless to say, to me and the guys, Bob was from that moment on known as Bolo. He didn't mind. He thought Bolo was kind of cool. Also, whenever we were in the pool and someone shouted "Marco", the proper response would forever be "Bolo!"

Bolo was a little bit different from the rest of us. He was almost a year younger because his birthday was in December. He always ended up being the youngest kid in our grade. He was the skateboarder in our group too. The rest of us were into baseball and football, but Bolo liked to skateboard and was into what we considered weird music, like David Bowie and The Cure. He'd always play baseball and football with us if he were there when a game started, but traditional sports weren't his thing. Consequently, he often seemed like a loner to us when he'd go off skateboarding by himself. Sometimes at night, you could hear the sound of his skateboard clattering to the street, when he was out under a streetlight practicing his flip kicks and ollies. He had a mullet and earring, and wore jeans and concert t-shirts while the rest of us were pretty clean cut and hung out in basketball shorts all summer. Secretly, I had always envied his mullet but was too afraid to get one because I didn't want to get teased by the guys, like the time I had come to school in my new parachute pants. I still thought they were awesome, but the guys didn't appreciate my sense of style and let me know it, loudly and often.

Bolo was also different because he was diabetic. It always seemed like he had to leave to eat or check his blood sugar right when things were getting fun. We got used to that and didn't hold it against him too much.

His family was a little bit different too. It was just him, his older brother Scott, and his dad. Their mom had left when Bolo was young. He couldn't remember exactly when, and she was never talked about in his house. He said he didn't really remember her, but he always seemed just a little sad. Not in any obvious way, but it was just a feeling I sort of sensed was there. I felt bad for him because his dad worked the evening shift at a local soda bottling plant so he and Scott mostly looked after themselves after school every day, until Scott got an after-school job busing tables. I suppose that was why Bolo could get away with skateboarding at night, after the rest of us had to be inside. Cliff was tall and athletic, but he didn't have a nickname, at least not yet. The guys tried, but nothing really stuck. Despite his full name being Clifford, none of the Big Red Dog references really resonated with us. Cliff didn't really pick up any nicknames until high school, and those were mostly sports related.

As for me, I didn't really have one either. I wanted a cool nickname, but you can't just nickname yourself, right? Cooper became Coop, and occasionally, when they were teasing me about not asking a girl out or something, it was Chicken Coop. That one never really became a daily thing though. There were also a few names related to bodily functions that they called me, before my doctor and parents figured out that I was lactose intolerant. Let's just say it's not easy being a twelve-year-old boy who farts a lot. Big Pooper Cooper was not exactly the super-hero name I would choose for myself. Of course, I was always hoping they'd nickname me Crockett after my favorite TV detective Sonny Crockett of <u>Miami Vice</u>.

We all grew up in the same idyllic, suburban neighborhood. The place was such a stereotype. It was situated about ten miles outside of a medium-sized city. All the houses in our housing development were built at the same time, and our parents had four different models to choose from. All the houses had nice, moderately sized front yards and slightly bigger backyards.

The neighborhood was shaped like a horseshoe, with the exception of a little fifty-yard thumb that sort of stuck off one of the corners, as if the builders had other plans but changed their minds. From the end of that thumb, there was a little trail through a tree line that separated the neighborhood from the athletic fields behind Homer Cortland Elementary School. If you looked to the right of the athletic fields and playground, you could also see

Friedhof Cemetery, which was right next to the school property.

I always thought that the placement of that cemetery was odd. Or more accurately, the placement of the elementary school was odd. When I was younger, I always found it more than a little disconcerting that there was a cemetery right next to our elementary school. Based on our discussions while we sat on the swings and watched funeral processions during recess, most of my friends found it as creepy as I did. If it was near dusk and one of us hit a baseball into Friedhof Cemetery, we would just leave it there. On a few occasions, that had ended our game because we usually only brought one ball.

We used to wonder which existed first, the cemetery or the elementary school. Then one bright, sunny summer afternoon, out of sheer boredom, we took a walk through that cemetery and really looked at the headstones for the first time. Of course, we had to tease and dare each other until we all agreed to go in. What we discovered was that the town and cemetery were far older than we had ever suspected. A few of the tombstones dated back to the early 1800s.

In our neighborhood, there were fifty-six houses in all. We knew this because the guys and I had counted them all on one of our many walks around the neighborhood when we were bored. Behind the neighborhood at the same end as the school, but over to the left as you came through the trail, was an open field that had actually been farmed a few years back but now was left alone, with nature slowly reclaiming it. Past that field was a small forest we called *"the woods"*. That was the official name we had given it. Everyone in the neighborhood knew where you were talking about when you said *the woods.*

To us though, it didn't seem like a small forest. *The woods* were sort of a magical kingdom for us. We had our beaten paths that took us from the neighborhood out to *the woods*. We had trails through the woods that only we knew about. We spent hours out there exploring, building "forts", climbing trees, playing hide and seek, and just sitting around our encampments talking and fantasizing about baseball, girls, adulthood, and whatever else young boys talked about. The older teens in the neighborhood had even put up a zip line between some trees, using some rope and a couple of clothesline wheels attached to a piece of wood for a handle.

It definitely wasn't the best or safest zip line in the world. It started about twenty feet up a tree, which we would climb. The line was probably about a hundred feet long. Once you sent yourself flying, hanging by just your grip on the wooden handle, you had to stop yourself by either putting your feet up and bouncing off the tree at the end, or you had to drop off about eight feet above the ground and hit this little slope beneath it just right. This was one of the many things that were probably better left unknown to our parents. So far though, no one had gotten seriously injured, so it was perfectly safe as far as we were concerned.

During our summer vacations, hours passed like minutes in our secret world. It truly was our world. As far back as I could remember, not a single adult had ever set foot in *the woods*. Even if they did, they would be lost because they didn't know our trails or hidey-holes. It was a big enough forest that on sunny days, it was darker and cooler in there beneath the thick, high branches. Although we felt like we were worlds away from the safe, bright neighborhood, we weren't so far that we couldn't hear our parents call our names from the back door when it was time for dinner.

The woods had their own lore as well. Rumors of ghosts or beasts spotted, of legendary fights between older brothers, amazing tales of surviving falls from the tallest trees and the like. We once spent an entire summer trying to find evidence to prove that _Bigfoot_ was roaming our woods, until we discovered that it was all a prank played on us by the older brothers in the neighborhood.

There was also the old well where one of the older boys claimed to have seen a human hand briefly float to the surface, before sinking back into the murky darkness. That totally creeped me out, and I was afraid to go anywhere near it for a whole summer. The stories never ended and they were, most of the time, all the product of our creative imaginations.

The biggest mystery of our woods was _The Sneaker Tree._ The tree itself wasn't extraordinary in any particular way. It was situated in the southeast corner of the woods amongst other trees. It wasn't overly tall or wide or of any exotic type that wasn't native to our part of the country. I think it might have been maple. It was tall enough that it had probably spent the last twenty years growing from seed to sapling to full-fledged, climb-worthy tree. We had never climbed it though. In fact, until five or six years ago, no one had noticed it.

It was the older boys in the neighborhood that noticed first. I think it was Bolo and Chuck's brothers who saw them. They were probably out in the woods smoking or something. They had come back to the neighborhood talking about sneakers on a tree. The guys and I went out to check it out and sure enough, there were two sneakers nailed to a tree about eight feet up. They looked like kids' sneakers, one a boys and one a girls. They weren't nailed up as if they were a pair. One was a little higher up and off to the side of the other one, as if they had been hurriedly and haphazardly put up there.

We didn't think too much of it at the time, but then the next summer we noticed another sneaker had been put up, and then a few weeks after that, another one appeared. That was when we started to wonder about *The Sneaker*

Tree. I'm not sure why, but it kind of creeped me out. Something just felt wrong about it. Once or twice a year, over the next couple of years, other sneakers would magically appear nailed to the tree. No one ever found any of their sneakers missing, so it was a mystery where the sneakers came from. *The Sneaker Tree* became another part of the lore of our woods, with all kinds of wild speculation about where the sneakers came from and who put them there.

Chapter 4

There was only a month of school left. I went through the daily motions, feeling as if I were swimming through a fog. It just felt wrong that, after a few days, everyone in school seemed to be going on with life as if nothing had happened. The school counselor tried to talk to me a few times, but I told her I was fine. I spent enough time thinking about Scooter. I didn't want to keep talking about him.

His locker was next to mine though. No one had bothered to take the Yankees sticker off it yet, so I saw it and thought of Scooter several times a day. That locker seemed like a shrine to Scooter just because of that sticker, and I imagined that his spirit or ghost might be trapped in there. I knew the combination, but I was too scared to look inside. The guys and I talked about Scooter a little bit now and then but in general, we avoided the topic. None of us seemed to know what to do with our feelings, so we just made fart jokes and pretended that it wasn't in our heads every day.

We had started practicing for the Little League season. That was my only refuge. The only thing that seemed to make my pulse quicken and made me feel alive, and maybe even a little happy. I seemed to be practicing well and hitting the ball pretty consistently. The coach,

Cliff's dad, even planned to let me pitch this year. It was all fine so far, as long as we didn't have to go to the field where Scooter had died.

Of course, we did though. In fact, my teams' first game of the season was on that field. Cliff's dad said that Cliff would start the game pitching, and I would be the closer if we needed one. I was thrilled and dismayed at the same time. Obviously, at twelve, I had no idea I was dismayed because at the time, I had no idea what that word meant. I just know I was anxious and afraid to set foot on that field. There was just a sense, a feeling of heavy foreboding, when I woke up that Saturday morning. I had no idea it was foreboding though. I was twelve.

We were the first game on the first day of the Little League season. They always did that on purpose. They always put the Yankees versus the Red Sox first, because where we lived, we were kind of on the invisible border where there were folks with loyalty to both major league teams. It was stupid though, because we were just the Mullane Motors Yankees playing against the Ho Jack Snack Shack Red Sox, and we all went to the same school.

It was a cool, sporadically rainy, late spring day. It was just miserable baseball weather, but unless there was lightning, they were going to let us play. We were the first game of the day, nine o'clock AM sharp. The field had been mown recently, and there were fresh lines, but the gray sky, cool temperatures, and rain put a damper on the general mood of everyone. In spite of the damp weather, there was a nice, little crowd of parents and family from both teams who had come to watch the game. Not my parents, of course.

Since I was in sixth grade this year, they had apparently decided that if the game was at the school at the end of our street, I could go on my own, and they didn't need to be there. I didn't think about it or feel slighted at the time. It's just the way it was.

As both teams and coaches lined up along the first and third baselines for the playing of the national anthem, something happened that I wasn't prepared for. Judging from the looks on my teammates faces, none of us was prepared for this.

I hadn't noticed her as I went through the warm-up drills with my teammates, but there she was, walking from home plate to the mound where her son had breathed his last breath. Scooter's mom was carrying a blue balloon and a baseball. Both sidelines respectfully became silent. Without a word from the public address announcer, or anyone, she stood on the mound, looked to the sky, and released the helium-filled balloon. After a few seconds of watching the balloon ascend, she did the sign of the cross. Then, standing on the white, rubber pitchers' stripe, she threw the ball to someone crouched as a catcher at the edge of the infield. I thought to myself that Scooter would be embarrassed if his mom had thrown the ball like that in front of him and all his friends. Her husband walked over from the third baseline, put his arm around her, and escorted her off the field. As they crossed the white line leaving the field, the P.A. announcer solemnly requested that everyone remove their hats and put their hands on their hearts for the national anthem. Then, as the last notes faded away, the P.A. announcer shouted, "*Play Ball!*"

The home and away designations for the game were always decided by a coin toss before the game. Cliff's dad had chosen Cliff and me to act as team captains for this game. It would be two different kids each game so that we all got a turn. Cliff's dad and the two of us walked to home plate to shake hands, hear the rules, and call the coin toss. "Heads!" Cliff shouted. It landed in the dirt next to home plate and, after a little roll, it fell with its heads side up. Personally, I liked the idea of being aggressive, taking the first at bats, and putting some runs on the board while your opponent still had a goose egg. Traditional baseball strategy though, called for taking the field first so that if you were behind in the final inning, you would get the last chance at-bats to come from behind. Cliff's dad was cool. He let the team captain choose first or second at-bats every game. He realized that it was just Little League, and he didn't stress about it too much like some parent coaches do. Cliff took it seriously though, and wanted to win every game, so he took the traditional route, and we took the field first.

Cliff took the mound, with Chuck behind the plate. I took my usual spot at second base. We had a girl, Andrea, at first base. The presence of a girl on the team had caused a little consternation amongst the guys when practices had started, but once we realized that she really was a good ballplayer and could hit a little bit, for a girl, we stopped worrying about it. Chuck even thought she was kind of cute and called dibs once. We never worried too much when Chuck called dibs. It rarely resulted in anything for him. Of course, I'd be pissed if she ever got to hit ahead of me in the lineup, but hopefully, that wouldn't ever happen.

This game was going to be a little tougher for our team than most. Not because of the competition, but because of something Cliff's dad had decided to do. He decided that in honor of Scooter, just for this one game, he would leave his name in our lineup. We all agreed that it would be a nice gesture to play one more game as if Scooter were with us. The problem for us in the game was that Little League rules dictated that if a batter was on the lineup card, but could not take his or her turn at bat, it would be an automatic out for the team each time that it was his turn. We all knew that, and we didn't care. We just decided that we'd play extra hard to compensate.

That game that day was unlike any game I had ever played. It was my dream game. Almost. It was like every ball I hit had eyes. In my first at bat, I was way too eager, and I lunged and swung at the first pitch I saw, even though it was probably outside the strike zone. I just wanted to hit, although I barely did that. It was a weak grounder up the third baseline. I hustled, digging and running for first. It was fielded perfectly, and he came up throwing. The ball and I appeared to reach first base at the same time. The umpire shouted, "Out. Out. No wait, safe!" just as my foot hit the front of the bag. What had looked like a perfect throw just tipped off the first baseman's glove, and Goob and Cliff, who had been on second and third, both scored.

Cliff was pitching a gem today. After two innings, he had four strikeouts. The other team couldn't seem to get a runner past first base. My second at bat was better as I settled into the game and relaxed a little. Cliff and Bolo had both gotten on board via walks and again, I was up with two outs and a chance to extend our lead with a good hit. The other team had switched pitchers already, and this kid was really throwing some heat. He blew the first pitch fastball by me, making me look silly as I flailed helplessly at it. I was down a strike, and I stepped out of the batter's box to gather myself, take a look at the third-base coach, Andrea's dad, and think about how I was going to try to hit this kid. Then just before I stepped back in, I saw him. Or thought I did anyway.

There was Scooter standing right next to the shortstop in a uniform that matched ours. At first, I thought it was one of our players leading off second base, until I remembered only Cliff was on first. I held up my hand to the ump to extend my respite a moment longer. I rubbed my eyes and looked again. There was only the opposing shortstop. Maybe I had just been imagining things. Shortstop was where Scooter usually played when he wasn't pitching. Anyway, he wasn't there now, so I stepped back into the box, dug in my cleats, and settled into my stance as the ump pointed to the pitcher.

He went into his wind up and before I could even take a breath, the ball was hurtling at me. Not at the catchers' mitt, but right at me. At my head. As I threw myself to the ground, I heard the ball just tip off the top of my bat. "Strike two!" the umpire shouted. It hardly seemed fair that I had to hit the dirt to keep my head from getting beaned, and I get a strike called on me. I got up, brushed the dirt off my uniform, and adjusted my helmet. I stepped back into the batters' box, settled into my stance, and waited for the pitch. This time, I could see it coming. A curveball. Not a good curveball the way the pros throw them, but a slow, rainbow curveball the way twelve-year-old pitchers throw them. It was perfect. It was like the ball was on a tee. I waited....

Then there was no thought on my part. I swung fast and hard. My bat met the ball perfectly. I could just feel the ball launch off the bat as I swung through. I dropped the bat and started running. I knew I had first if it wasn't caught, but it still hadn't come down as I rounded first and the coach was waving at me to keep running. Between first and second, I slowed down a little to turn my head to see where the ball went. To be honest, the idea of hitting my first home run passed through my mind at that moment. In the very next moment, I was deeply disappointed as I heard the ball hit the outfield fence. As I rounded second, the coach yelled, "Three. Three!" signaling that he wanted me to go for third. "Down, down!" he shouted at me as I approached. I had to slide. They were making the throw, trying to get me out. As I dropped to slide, I saw the ball hit his glove. He still had to make the tag. As the glove swept towards my foot, it appeared I might lose this race. My foot had to hit the bag before his glove hit me. It was going to be close. Then just as the glove touched my knee, the ball popped out and I was safe. A triple and another run batted in. Damn, this was a good day so far.

Once the dust had settled, the pitcher set up to pitch to Chuck. First pitch, ball. Second pitch, strike. Then the third pitch hit the dirt and skittered through, past the catcher, rolling all the way to the backstop. I scored from third easily.

Chapter 5

"Mom! Dad! I'm home!" I shouted as I walked in the front door and dropped my equipment. I was so excited to tell them about my great game.

"Don't you dare leave your stuff there!" she screeched at me. Geez, not even a "Hi Cooper, how was your game?" Typical. "Pick those up and take them to the laundry room. They're filthy," she continued at the same ear-splitting volume. I didn't see my dad anywhere. *He must be downstairs in his workshop*, I thought. That's where he always takes refuge when they're fighting. It was also where he had a fridge that usually had an ample supply of Genesee Cream Ale. How he never cut off a finger when he was drinking and woodworking was a miracle. As kids, you always see your parents' behavioral patterns. Sometimes you don't realize it, but how often do you remember just knowing what your parents were going to do in certain situations?

As much as I wanted to talk about my game, I wasn't going to bother either of them. I just went to my room and closed the door. After changing out of my baseball uniform, I lay on my bed, throwing my game ball up to the ceiling and catching it with the same hand. Over and over, I tried to get that perfect toss where it just brushed the ceiling before falling back to my hand. I had to be really careful though, because if my parents heard the ball hitting the ceiling or the floor, I would get yelled at. This was my way of meditating, I guess. I didn't think about it, but I guess I almost always seemed to do that when I was hiding in my room, trying to avoid the tension that my parents fighting caused. On days like this, when they had been arguing and were not on speaking terms, I thought I could actually feel the tension in the air. It was like a silent weight just sort of hanging there, unseen and unspoken. As long as it remained unspoken, I was good.

After about an hour or so, I figured it might be safe to leave my room. I just shouted, "I'm going over to Cliff's house," and then I left without waiting for a response or questions. I was pretty sure that there wouldn't be any anyway. I knew I could always find refuge at Cliff's house. He had a big family, and they never seemed to mind when I dropped in. I don't know if his parents suspected what was going on at my house and took pity, or if they just genuinely didn't mind me spending so much time there. It would be hard to believe they didn't know a little bit of what might be going on at my house. We lived next door and on a quiet summer night, shouting can carry.

Either way, I was thankful that they and Cliff were next door. They were like the family I wished I had. Everyone seemed happy to see me, and in all the time I spent there, I don't think I ever heard anyone utter a cross word. We had burgers on the grill that night, and the kids ate outside on the picnic table. After dinner, Cliff and I walked around, just sort of picking up the guys as we went. We didn't do anything special. We just walked a few laps of the neighborhood, talking about our game. We made a quick stop at the corner store at the end of the street to grab some snacks as we walked. As usual though, when the streetlights came on, it was time to head home.

As we walked past our houses, each member of our group would say his "see ya' later" and peel off to his house. When I walked into my house it was still silent, but not a good silent. You know how you can feel a bad silence? I could feel that malignant electric tension in the air. No one was yelling, but no one was around either. They were still not speaking, which sometimes felt worse than when they were yelling. I assumed that Dad might still be in his workshop and that Mom was in her room, reading. I headed straight for my room and closed the door behind me.

In general, I had always been a good kid. No serious troubles in school other than maybe a call home once a year for fooling around a little too much during the lockdown drill or something. At home, I did chores, didn't talk back, and got home when I was supposed to most of the time. I usually didn't give my parents too much reason to worry about me. Then again, they seemed so self-involved, I wasn't sure that they would worry about me anyway. I don't know if this was kind of sociopathic thinking, but at that moment, I thought to myself that it was great that I had built up enough trust that I could probably get away with stuff when I wanted to. This was one of those times.

Chapter 6

My window slid open quietly, and I lifted the screen. Fortunately for me, my parents had chosen the ranch-style house when they moved into the neighborhood. I lowered myself down onto the picnic table that was conveniently behind the house and beneath my window. I slowly pulled the screen back into place. I hoped that with the lights off, the pile of laundry I had placed under my covers would look like me if my parents peeked into my room. I stood for a moment and breathed in the cool night. I could taste the slight dampness of dew in the air. Other than the crickets, it appeared to be a quiet night. The lightning bugs were just starting to emerge. There would be more in a few weeks, but for now, there was still enough to make me think they looked like twinkling Christmas lights in the line of trees behind our house.

Despite the darkness, I knew exactly where the gap in the bushes was that would allow me to slip through to the well-worn trail that ran behind the tree line, parallel to our street. I had no worries about meeting neither man nor beast back there. I knew the trail like the back of my hand, and there was enough moonlight that I found my way easily to the baseball field. I clambered over the fence and just stood there for a moment, taking in another deep breath. I found the tranquility of the night soothing. In the moonlight, the field still seemed as perfect as it did on any summer day.

I walked over to the spot where my hit ball had hit the outfield fence. I touched the spot where I thought it had hit on the town Little League sign and silently cursed my bad luck. There was still a little dent where the ball had hit it. *Eighteen inches*! *I was eighteen inches away from my first home run. Damn it. Who knows if I'll ever get that precious combination of the perfect pitch and the perfect swing at the same time again*? That's the way life is. Sometimes you only get one chance and inches or split seconds separate success from failure.

I felt different than I had at the beginning of our game this morning. Gone was the tension and worry. Gone were the depressing thoughts about Scooter. I felt at home. I felt all the stress of the day melt away as I stood there breathing in the smell of grass and gazing across the field. I walked towards the infield. When I got to the pitcher's mound, I took my place on the pitching stripe, or the rubber as it was sometimes called. I was still too embarrassed to call it that, but occasionally the adults did, and all of us kids had to suppress giggles. I remember once during a game last year when Cliff stepped off the mound to talk to the infielders and from the dugout his dad yelled, 'C'mon Clifford, get back on the rubber. You're holding up the game!" We all broke out laughing as we trotted back to our positions, and I could see Cliff blushing as he went into his wind up. Of course, he threw that pitch into the dirt about three feet in front of home plate. I had to hold my glove in front of my face to hide my laughter.

I exhaled and could see my breath in the cool, damp night air as I threw a few fake pitches towards home plate. Each one a perfect strike, of course. *It can't hurt to practice my pitching motion*, I thought to myself. *I'm probably going to pitch more this year. I wonder if Don Johnson pitched as a kid. Or Sonny Crockett. I bet he did. He seems like he'd be pretty cool on the mound.* After throwing a few more from the stretch and practicing my throw over to first to catch the imaginary runner there, I decided to take a few invisible swings as well.

I approached home plate and stepped into the batter's box with my invisible bat held above my shoulder. I dug in and pictured a pitcher there on the mound, going into his wind up. At first, I was just imagining any pitcher, but as I dug my feet in a little and looked up at the mound, I saw him again. It was Scooter. He was going into his wind up just like he did on that fateful day when he threw his last pitch, only this time he was pitching to me. As the imaginary ball approached I loaded my weight on my back leg, drove my hands downward, keeping them inside the ball as my hips turned and my weight shifted towards my front leg, driving the bat head level through the zone. My follow through was perfect, causing my top hand to release like Daryl Strawberry did as the bat came around. Scooter turned to watch the invisible ball fly and shook his head like a pitcher who had just given up the game winner. I trotted the bases and when I made it back to home, Scooter was there.

He appeared to be waiting for a high five, which I attempted to give him, but my hand met no resistance, although I did feel something like a tremor where my hand contacted his in the air. I felt a little lightheaded. I wasn't sure if it was from my run around the bases or something else. "Scooter," I said tentatively, "what are you doing here?"

He looked at me and shrugged his shoulders. 'I don't know," he said. "I've been here since I died. I can't leave." When he spoke, there was no visible breath from condensation in the air as there had been when I spoke. Was I imagining this? Was it real? Was I going crazy?

"So you're a ghost?" I said. "How awesome is that? This is so cool! I still get to see you!" Scooter just looked at me. Although he looked kind of solid, he also didn't look exactly right at the same time either.

"Uh… Coop. I hate to break it to ya' but I'm still dead, I think. I mean, don't get me wrong, it's great to see you. I was worried no one would ever see me or talk to me and I'd be stuck here like this forever," he replied. We walked as we talked, ending up in the dugout where we both sat down. I don't know if I was loopy or what, but I couldn't stop chattering away at Scooter, or his ghost, or my imagination.

"So you've been here this whole time? Did you see my game today? Three hits! I almost put one out!"

"Um yeah, well, of course I saw it. Funny how those two balls just popped out of their gloves, wasn't it?" Scooter said. I was so self-centered that I completely missed his implication. It could also be that ghosts are just terrible at facial expressions and tone of voice. "Thanks for leaving me in the lineup though," Scooter said. "I ran the bases." My brain just felt like it was going to explode. Like I said, I wasn't sure if I was crazy, or if I was back in my room dreaming all this, but I didn't mind for now. It was great to be able to talk to Scooter again.

We sat and talked for another hour or so. He asked about school, and I caught him up on everything he had missed. As it got later though, I worried my parents might discover my escape and call the police or something. "Look Scooter, I've got to go before I get into trouble. Will you be here tomorrow?" I asked.

"I don't know. I hope so," he replied. Then a thought occurred to me.

"Hey Scooter," I said, "Why do ghosts always play baseball?" He looked at me like I was crazy, which was entirely possible.

"What are you talking about?" he said.

"You know," I replied, "like in all those movies. Why are ghosts always playing baseball? Do you think there are ghosts playing football somewhere? How about soccer? Are there ghost soccer players too?"

He laughed. "Shut up, you idiot! Great! The one alive person I get to talk to, and these are the questions I get? Get out of here before your parents miss you. Although, I doubt they would." I thought for a moment that Scooter looked apologetic immediately after saying that, but it was hard to tell. Like I said, ghosts aren't that good at facial expressions.

I couldn't help but ask one last question before I went. "Well, what do you do at night when no one is here?" Scooter appeared to think for a moment.

"I'm not sure. I don't really remember. I can't remember where I am except for when living people are here. I'll try to be here tomorrow."

Chapter 7

The next morning... That's when the terror began. "Did you hear?" Goob asked.

"No. Hear what?" I asked.

"The murder!" he exclaimed. "She was found in Friedhof Cemetery. A girl. I heard my parents talking about it. Wanna go see?" Did I want to go see? That was a stupid question. We cut through the trail and made our way to the baseball field. When we got there, we could see police cars and a coroner's van in the cemetery, Cops were milling about. We stayed on the baseball field, afraid to go any closer.

We watched for a while. I'm not sure what we hoped to see. After a bit, Bolo joined us too. "You guys see anything?" he asked. We both shook our heads.

"Do you know who it was?" I asked. He shook his head as well. Arms folded, we all leaned on the outfield fence. Last night's encounter with Scooter was far from my mind.

A murder in our quaint little suburb was unthinkable. Nothing like this had ever happened here as far as I knew. We were a slice of Americana. Corner store. Kids playing ball in the street. Neighbors that knew each other. Nothing like this was supposed to happen here. Murders and kidnappings happened in the city, or at least that was my perception of the world. Our parents ordered us to stay out of the woods and not to go anywhere alone.

On the news that evening, I heard a little bit more about the murder. It was a ten-year-old girl. Her body left in the cemetery. Not a mark on it and no apparent cause of death, but she was dead just the same. She had taken her dog out to pee one last time for the night and never returned. The dog was found whining on the back porch a little while later, his leash still attached, trailing behind him. According to the news report, a handwritten note had been left under the body. It read, *"Roses are red and violets are blue, if you don't catch me, there will be two."* The police were reportedly "pursuing leads".

I suddenly felt a chill run through my veins as I realized that the murder had happened last night. I was here at the baseball field last night by myself. I didn't see or hear anything, but I wondered, could it have been me? What if I, out here at night by myself, had crossed the killer's path? I was alone, and no one knew where I was last night. That could have been me. I couldn't tell the guys though. My story about Scooter would just sound too weird. They'd make fun of me and call me crazy. We already had the one guy in the neighborhood we were sure was crazy, or at least creepy. Like every neighborhood, we had our cast of stereotypical characters, including the neighborhood crazy guy, or creeper as we called him.

According to the stories, after dropping out of high school, the creeper, Greg Genzler, had joined the army and gone to war. After his time was up, he returned to live with his father down the street, about four or five houses past Chuck. I had never seen him doing anything "crazy," but it did creep us all out that he seemed to stare quite a bit. If he was out mowing the lawn or standing on his porch smoking a cigarette as we walked by on the street, he didn't offer a friendly wave, just a stare as we passed his house. Not an angry stare, just a stare. It wasn't just us either. Everyone in the neighborhood had gotten *The Genzler stare-down.*

Weirdly, although he was creepy and, in our minds, the number-one murder suspect, we were still jealous of his hair. He had one of those awesomely cool haircuts, where it was kind of long in the back and short on the front and sides. Once Chuck had actually uttered the phrase "business in the front and party in the back", and he had received several charley horses from us for sounding like such a dork. Years later, we would mock the mullet after we had cut ours off, but when we were twelve, we were so jealous of *Genzler's* hair because none of our parents would let us grow the back long. *Genzler* may have been crazy as a shithouse rat, but at least he had that hair going for him.

Once, however, a story started circulating via the neighborhood grapevine that he had apparently walked into a stranger's house in another neighborhood, because he had heard someone calling him. He didn't do anything threatening or crazy as the story went, but it became part of our neighborhood lore just the same, and Genzler was, in our minds, the neighborhood crazy guy. That's what we called him, *Genzler*. It sounded kind of sinister and fitting to us. You never hear about a psychopath named Greg, right? It had to be *Genzler*. *Genzler* just had an evil ring to it for us. That's why I couldn't tell the guys about seeing Scooter last night. I didn't want to be the neighborhood crazy guy in waiting, or worse yet, a suspect in the murder.

The next day at school, we found out who she was. Everyone was talking about it. Amanda Arseneau had been a fourth grader at Homer Cortland Elementary School. She didn't live in our neighborhood, but lived on the next street over. I didn't know her of course, but I knew who her brother was. He was in fifth grade, a year behind me, and on another team in our town Little League. At both schools, they had assembly meetings in the auditorium, where the principal gave all the facts that he could appropriately give and discussed the need for everyone to be in by dark and never to go anywhere without a companion. As usual, school counselors would be available for us to talk to.

This was the next to last week of school. After Friday, I'd only have to go back a few specific times next week to take finals. I just wanted this year to be over. I just wanted to drift into the seemingly never-ending days of summer where we slept in, went swimming all day, hung out with friends, and hopefully, weren't reminded of death too often.

That afternoon, after school, the guys and I grabbed our baseball bats and, instead of heading out to the ball field, we took the trail to the woods. We imagined that we were total bad asses that could take down a killer if we needed to. Our grandiose bravado knew no bounds. We didn't have a plan. We were just going to hang out in the woods. We rarely went out there with any plan to do anything. We climbed trees, deciding which ones would suffice as lookout posts if we were to spot the killer. We sat on our circle of rocks and logs and planned where we would hide, or how we would ambush the killer if he were to be so unlucky as to try to hide out in our woods. It never once occurred to us that any one of us could possibly become a victim. Such was the naïve hubris of twelve-year-old boys.

"Goob, are you kidding me?" I teased, "You can't use a baseball bat for what it's intended for, much less for what it's not. You better be our lookout up in the tree." The guys all laughed. It wasn't mean spirited. It was just the way we talked to each other. I was sure that I'd get mine in return from one of the guys.

"Guys, this is serious," Cliff said. "We can't be screwing around. The cemetery isn't too far away; the killer could easily be hiding out here." Cliff was an interesting twelve year old. One minute he would be as goofy as the rest of us and dishing out as much abuse as anyone and in the next minute, he could be 'serious as a heart attack' as they say. That wasn't a bad thing either, because the rest of us were full-on idiots almost all the time.

Chuck had brought his brother's B.B. gun. "Hey, be careful Chuck, you'll shoot your eye out!" Bolo laughed so hard when he said this, that he fell off the log he was sitting on and lay on the ground laughing.

We all started laughing, not at his joke, but at how hard he was laughing, when, suddenly, Cliff held his hand up and said, "Shhhhh… listen…" Towards the southeast corner of the woods, we heard a "crack" and a few birds took off through the trees. There was a scamper in the underbrush, not big enough to be a person, but something had startled the wildlife over there.

We all sat, frozen in place, for at least the next two to three minutes. The longer we sat there in silence, listening to nothing more than the crickets, the more I felt the goose bumps rise on my skin. I imagined I was sensing something, but in reality, I was just scared to death. We all had our eyes wide open, slowly turning our heads from side to side, eyes occasionally meeting. Chuck had his B.B. gun up as he looked around, as if he were prepared to deal the killer a nasty little B.B. shaped welt if he dared to show himself. To be honest, I was more worried that he'd put my eye out with an errant shot fired off in a panic.

Just as we were beginning to relax, the sudden, loud crack of a stick breaking reverberated throughout the woods. We all froze again. I looked across the circle at Bolo, and his eyes were big and black, almost all pupils, just like my cat gets when he's stalking something. I knew Bolo wasn't stalking anything. He was as terrified as I was that we were the ones being stalked. Looking around our little circle, I could tell we were all just as scared.

Cliff motioned for us all to stand up quietly. We all obeyed slowly and silently. Then he motioned for us to follow him. In a line, we all began to slowly creep towards the main trail that would lead us out of the woods. Our baseball bats were still in our hands, but they seemed useless against an enemy we couldn't see and who, in our imaginations, was the epitome of evil. At least that was what was in my imagination. To be honest, I was glad I had already taken a leak over in the old well in the woods before we had settled into our talk. I don't care what the circumstances were—if you peed your pants in front of your friends, they would never let you forget it.

As we made it to the main path, I heard a "whoosh" somewhere just above us and something came hurtling through the branches, crashing into the underbrush to my left. Then something hit the tree to our right. Behind us, there was suddenly a tremendous thrashing and growling sound coming from a thicket of bushes and trees. I turned my head to look and saw branches moving. "RUN!" Cliff shouted. That instruction was hardly necessary, as most of us were already in motion, dashing up the trail towards the doorway of light that signified the opening into the open field. In my little brain, that light meant safety.

Arms and knees pumping as hard as they could, we all were running, trying our best not to trip or run over or into each other. Bolo fell once, but got up so quickly that he was still in front of me. I dropped my baseball bat, worried that it would slow me down. I didn't care. I just didn't want to be last. I imagined that behind me was some voracious monster with sharp, bloody claws and jagged teeth gnashing as it nipped at my heels. I know it was all in my imagination, but I thought I could hear the breathing of some great beast, and it sounded like it was gaining on me.

Cliff made the opening first, and we all quickly followed, but we didn't stop there. We all ran another fifty yards before Cliff stopped and held up his hand. We all stopped and tried to catch our breath, as we turned to look towards the woods to see if we had been pursued. What we saw when we turned around made our faces collectively drop. Standing at the opening to the main trail into the woods was Bolo's older brother Scott, Goob's big brother, and Chuck's older brother Don, and they were laughing their asses off.

Chapter 8

The last week of classes was different from usual. Of course, it being my first year in the middle school, I wasn't sure what to expect, but the mood was very subdued. It was hard to be happy about school being almost done, when there was constant news coverage about the funeral and rumors and stories regarding the killer were rampant. Because of the note, they were calling him *The Poetry Killer*. There were police officers at all the elementary and middle schools to monitor arrival and departure each day. Teachers were checking students in and out of classrooms in addition to the usual hall passes. We were in junior high, and they were even making the boys go to the bathroom in pairs!

With school being tense and home being tense, it was hard to concentrate on finals and again, baseball and "the guys" became my refuge. After school, we all headed to the ball field to practice for tomorrow's game. Our folks didn't really worry too much. At least mine didn't. As far as they were concerned, if I was with the guys, everything was just fine. As I grabbed my stuff to leave for the field, I couldn't find my bat. Then I remembered. "Crap!" I said aloud to myself as I recalled dropping it as I fled the woods the other day. *Shit. I guess I'll just have to borrow one today*, I thought to myself.

I made a point not to cut through the tree line and take the trail to the field alone. I wasn't scared mind you, just obeying my parents. I went down the street and took the little trail off the corner that led straight into the baseball field behind the elementary school. I was the last to get there this time. As I walked up behind Chuck, who was playing catch with Goob, I heard him say, "So do you really think there's a serial killer around here?" Goob saw me coming, but Chuck didn't, and just a fraction of a second after he released his throw to Gooby, I brought my hands down on his shoulders and yelled "Ha!" He startled and jumped so quickly that we all burst out laughing. I even fell to the ground.

"Ha ha, real funny Cooper! Trust me, you'll get yours when you least expect it," Chuck exclaimed as he threw his glove at me while I rolled on the ground, laughing so hard that I had to catch my breath. To be honest, I think Chuck was more embarrassed because Andrea was there for practice today, and he wanted to impress her. I guess I should have been more sensitive, but then again, I was twelve and yelling "Ha" was about as sensitive as I got. I felt bad though, because I saw him look in Andrea's direction right after he threw his glove at me. I noticed that she was the only one not laughing at Chuck.

Interesting, I thought to myself.

There were only seven of us. The rest of the guys we usually played with weren't able to leave the neighborhood without their parents until the serial killer was captured. Fortunately for the guys and me, our parents weren't quite as restrictive, because they knew how tight knit we were and trusted that we would always be together. It would have to be a four on three game, with a couple of ghost runners and fielders. Chuck, Cliff, and I would take on Andrea, Goob, Bolo, and Romeo. Whoever was on deck to hit would have to play catcher.

Bolo called pitcher, while Andrea grabbed her customary position at first. Goob took second. Romeo kind of played shortstop and third base at the same time. I stepped into the batter's box first and on the first pitch, I laced a beautiful single to right field and made first base easily. I loved stealing bases, but since we were short on players, we ruled out base stealing because of the chaos that ensued if there was an errant throw. We also ruled out walks since we had no umpires. If you swung, it was a strike, a foul ball, or a hit. If you didn't swing, it didn't count as anything, but each at bat was limited to six pitches. The general consensus was that if you couldn't get on base with six pitches, you were a moron and didn't deserve to get on base anyway.

Chuck came up, and popped out, but I tagged up and made it to second. Cliff got up to bat and hit a grounder that found the hole between first and second. Cliff was on first, and I was on third, but it was my turn at bat again. "Ghost runner," I shouted as I trotted over to the dugout and grabbed a bat. When I turned around to walk to the batter's box, I saw him again. Scooter was on third. He was literally the ghost runner. I laughed a little and shook my head. "You won't be laughing in a minute when I strike you out," Bolo shouted at me good-naturedly. "Get in the batter's box and take your punishment."

I stepped into the batter's box and settled into my stance. First pitch I saw, I swung at and hit it good. I thought it might even go out. As I ran to first, I looked over and saw Scooter race home from third and slide unnecessarily into home plate with a flourish. Maybe only I saw it, or maybe it was in my imagination, but I could have sworn I saw a little dust kick up when he slid. I turned my head back to watch the flight of my magnificent shot and slowed up as I saw it hit the warning track and bounce over the fence. Ground rule double. Damn. Cliff only got third. "One nothing," I shouted. "How'd that feel, Bolo?"

It was a warm, dry, late June day so we kept playing. Scooter stayed on the field as our ghost runner and fielder. It's too bad only I could see him. My friends had to think I was nuts as I laughed throughout at Scooter's antics.

One time when a fly ball was hit in his direction, he would have fielded it perfectly had he been a live player. After it passed through his glove, he mimed looking at his glove as if it might have a hole in it. Another time as I was up to bat, he walked up behind Bolo on the pitcher's mound and pretended to pull his shorts down. Bolo caught me laughing and crowed a little after getting one of his weak fastballs by me for a strike.

"Hey, you kids," a voice shouted from the other side of the right field fence. "You gotta get going! It's going to get dark soon. It ain't safe here." It was Mr. Gregersen, the elementary school janitor. "You kids need to get home. With that killer running around, you can't be out here." He apparently felt it necessary to break up our fun even when we weren't in school. Unbelievable. He had walked all the way over to the outfield fence from the staff parking lot. Geez, what did he care? He had never seemed to most of us like he even liked the kids. He was always yelling at us. In my eyes, he seemed like "Old Man Jenkins" from the <u>Scooby Doo</u> cartoons. If he had also shouted, "I would have gotten away with it too if it weren't for you meddling kids and your dog," as he shook his fist at us, I wouldn't have been surprised. That dude is so old that my mom says he was the janitor here when she went to school. Doesn't every elementary school have a guy like him?

Bolo definitely didn't like him though. Bolo was still holding a grudge from the time in fourth grade when he grabbed him by the arm and dragged him down to the principal's office after he had made the water fountain squirt water all over Gooby. He had grabbed Bolo's arm hard. *Too hard,* I thought, *kind of like he took a little delight in causing just that tiny twinge of pain.* It still makes Bolo furious to think about it, but the principal and his dad wouldn't listen because he had been the one fooling around in the hall.

I know Mr. Gregersen seemed like the stereotypical grumpy old guy who hated kids and would probably take our ball if we ever accidentally hit one into his yard, but he was ok with me and always would be. We lived in a relatively small town and in elementary school, gossip travels fast, especially if it's really embarrassing to someone. Last year I had an 'incident' that would have been the talk of the school and probably followed me for a long time, but neither the guys nor anyone else ever found out about it, thanks to Mr. Gregersen. One day last year, before my doctor figured out that I was lactose intolerant, I had chocolate milk with lunch. A short while later I was paired with Claire Simmons, the girl of my dreams, for a science project.

The combination of my nervousness around Claire, and my digestive system's animosity towards lactose, all came to a head at the same time. I started to feel a familiar rumbling in my lower intestines, and I knew what would come next. Without even asking permission, I hurried from the class to find the nearest restroom. Unfortunately, I didn't make it in time. My pants were a mess, and I was stuck hiding in a restroom stall for twenty minutes before, as luck would have it, Mr. Gregersen came in to mop. He snuck me down to the locker room before the change of classes. While I showered, he went to the nurse's office to get me some clean pants from the lost and found. As I thanked him and headed back to class with a pass he had procured from the nurse, he nodded and said, "Don't worry. It's our secret."

"I gotta get going anyway guys," Andrea said, "We might as well quit now. You guys had no chance to beat us anyway," she said with a smile. This brought a little bit of laughter all around because our side had been up by a score of 12-2 or something like that.

As we broke up and everyone went their separate directions, I decided I'd take a detour through the woods on my way home before it got too dark. I wanted to find my baseball bat before the older kids did. I knew that if they found it, I'd never get it back. I didn't want to have to explain to my dad that I had lost the bat he bought for me. Sadly, I feared my dad more than I did *The Poetry Killer*.

Cliff saw me leaving in the direction of the trail towards the woods and shouted, "Hey Coop, where ya' going?" I replied that I was going to get my bat before it was too dark and before the older kids stole it. He offered to go with me, but I shrugged him off. I figured I'd only be a minute. I knew exactly where I had dropped it. I just had to follow the main trail that we had come running out of the woods on. I left the baseball field and headed up the trail towards the woods. The sun wasn't due to set for at least another half hour, so I thought to myself that I should be fine. As I approached the woods, I was completely in shadow as the towering trees had blocked the sun before it had reached the horizon elsewhere.

I suddenly felt very nervous. I could feel goose bumps rising on my skin and the hair on the back of my neck standing on end as I approached the entrance to the woods. During the bright light of the day, this place was as comfortable as home. I knew every inch like the back of my hand. I was going to have to. It was dark in there. I took a deep breath and crossed the crest of the little hill that was at the mouth of the entrance to the woods. Almost immediately, I was enveloped in darkness. I stopped and waited for my eyes to adjust. They did, but there's only so much you are physically capable of seeing when it's dark.

During the day when I was out here with my friends, and we could see the sunlight filtering through the trees or illuminating the entrance trail, the dimness in the forest was somehow comforting. Here, at night, when I was by myself, it felt malevolent, menacing. I'm sure it was my imagination, but knowing that still didn't make me feel any better.

With my vision limited by the lack of lighting, I paused to listen. It sounded much like it did during the day. A chorus of crickets was serenading me. I could hear the occasional chirping or chattering of birds above. Occasionally, there was a scamper through the underbrush. I appeared to be alone. I turned and looked back at the bright opening at the head of the trail just to reassure myself. Somewhere in the distance, I thought I heard the music of the ice-cream truck as it trolled the neighborhood for business.

If I just followed the trail straight ahead about thirty yards or so, I should find my bat by the side of the trail where I had tossed it as I fled in terror yesterday. I moved ahead slowly, trying to make as little noise as possible. Each footstep was carefully placed. My ears felt as if they were actually turning, like cats do, to monitor for any sound that shouldn't be there. I wanted to hurry, but I knew that to do so could be disastrous.

I was about thirty yards into the woods, and neither my vision, nor feeling around the trail with my feet, had located the missing bat. I had made it right to where we had turned onto the main trail from where we had been sitting. I knew this because I remember being careful not to run into that stump as I ran helter-skelter for safety. The bat had to be somewhere over there in the underbrush, between the trail and where we had made our little circle to talk. I shuffled my feet through the underbrush in the direction I thought we had come from yesterday. The light was fading, and the woods seemed to fall silent. I could hear my breathing. I kept a very careful and slow shuffle as I moved.

Finally, as I got to our little knights of the roundtable circle of logs and rocks, I felt my toe bump something. I crouched and reached down, feeling about for the bat. As I did so, I heard the sound of footsteps coming up the path, footsteps that weren't worried about being heard. I was sure it was the killer, and I was sure my body would be found in the cemetery tomorrow.

I froze, as much out of fear and uncertainty as any self-protective instincts. I stayed in my crouch, not moving, trying to hold my breath as I listened. My view of the trail was mostly blocked by bushes and trees. The footsteps came closer. Now they sounded no more than fifteen feet away. Then, my worst fear was realized. The footsteps slowed.

I held my breath. I wanted to turn my head or move a little to try to get a better view. My legs began cramping. I felt on the verge of collapse, lungs burning, legs on the verge of giving out, when it happened. I hadn't meant it too. It just slipped out. I farted. I couldn't help it. *The Telltale Fart*, I thought to myself. Then I had to stifle a giggle. That wasn't hard when I saw the shadowy figure stop in his tracks. I think he heard me.

Suddenly, there was a bright orange flash. Whoever it was had stopped to light a cigarette. After it was lit, he appeared to crouch down to pick something up. I guess I was assuming it was a he. I had never heard of a girl serial killer. As I remained crouched, I risked letting out a little breath and inhaled through my nose. The dry, stale smell of cigarette smoke hung in the damp air. Thank God he hadn't seen me when his lighter briefly illuminated the area around him.

My vision was obscured by my vantage point, and I was only able to only able to make out the shadowy shape of a human figure through gaps in the leaves. It was like watching that old, grainy Bigfoot footage. Then I saw what he had picked up. The shadowy outline of a human shape now included a baseball bat in his right hand. *Sonofabitch!* I thought to myself. *That emm effer has my bat! And he's walking away with it! My good bat. Fuck!* Of course, I said this in my head. Not because I was afraid of the serial killer, but because I was twelve, and was too timid to swear out loud. Ok, maybe I was a little afraid of the serial killer.

I moved a little to relieve the cramping in my legs, but I waited. *Oh my effing God!* I screamed in my mind. *There's a mosquito on my ear*! This little field trip was not going well. I literally gritted my teeth as it finally landed, and I had to sit there and let it bite my ear and drink my blood. I'm sure the real physical pain was negligible, but the psychological pain of being helpless to stop it was driving me insane.

After about five minutes without another sound in the woods, I risked rising to an upright position. It appeared that I was alone. The normal forest noises had returned. I felt a little anxious about my prospects on the walk home without my baseball bat. I may not be much of a fighter, but I was pretty damn good at hitting things with a metal bat.

When I got home, I could feel that tension hanging in the air again. Mom was in the kitchen tensely doing dishes, and Dad was in his recliner with a glass of whiskey and the newspaper. Since I was pretty sure there wasn't going to be a family dinner, I made myself a sandwich and went to my room to eat while I watched TV. From the kitchen, my mom asked, "Cooper, do you have any homework?"

"No, Mom, "I answered. "It's the last week; we're only reviewing for finals." This seemed to satisfy her. I had that feeling like I always did. It had been a great day, until I got home. I had no insight. I just knew how I felt. Even if they weren't overtly yelling at each other or me, I could still tell when things weren't good, and that was happening more and more lately. I wish I could talk to Scooter. He was who I usually leaned on in the past. His parents didn't get along great either, so we would usually compare notes to see who had the worst situation. It was pretty close to a draw most of the time.

I asked my dad to play a game of chess. He had been teaching me lately, and I really liked it. He usually beat me pretty handily after stringing me along for a bit, but I didn't mind. Each game I seemed to hang in there a little longer, and I was starting to see and feel the rhythm of the game. I wasn't very good yet, but I was starting to understand how my dad was manipulating me and moving me around the board by provoking my reactive moves, until he had me in position to go for the kill. Unfortunately, tonight he just gave a grunt and mumbled something about being too tired to play.

The summer sitcom re-runs had started and there was nothing good to watch, so I headed to my room. That was the one place in the house I could hang out where I couldn't feel the tension. I re-read a couple Spider-Man comic books and played a bit on my Atari. I was still feeling antsy. I just couldn't relax. With it being a school night, I knew my parents wouldn't let me go out now that it had gotten dark. As usual, it didn't matter to Bolo. I could hear his skateboard outside in the street. He was no doubt under the streetlight at the corner, practicing his kick-flips and "ollies". He had tried to teach me once when I had taken a brief interest in skateboarding, but I didn't stick with it long enough to get the hang of anything other than gliding forward in a straight line.

Chapter 9

My dad was a news guy. Every weekend morning, I'd come down the hall to find him in his recliner with a cup of coffee and the newspaper. A local news channel was usually on the TV. I'm not sure why, but he was also fascinated by the weather. He had to know the weather. All day, every day… if you needed to know what the weather was going to do in the next few hours, he was your man. He left the house every day completely prepared for whatever the weather might bring. I, on the other hand, to this day, still leave the house only prepared for the weather I want. In the evenings, he'd settle into the same recliner with a glass of scotch whiskey instead of coffee as he watched the evening news programs.

I wasn't much for watching the news myself. At twelve, I generally had little respect for the local news. In my mind, the local news had nothing interesting to say, and was usually just trying to attach some local angle to a national or worldwide story. Our sleepy little suburb had never been mentioned in the news before as far as I knew. As of this week however, the murder of Amanda Arseneau was the top story on the local news, as the police worked feverishly to capture the murderer that the local and national news media had taken to calling *The Poetry Killer.*

Oh my god, that is awful, I thought to myself. *The Poetry Killer?* Jeez, adults are corny. That's as bad as how they name hurricanes. They name a category-five hurricane something like Sandy or Lisa, and then they expect people to flee their homes as if their life depended on it? I might flee from Hurricane Deathtron, but Hurricane Lisa, probably not. *The Poetry Killer* was just as corny. *Seriously*, I thought, *who is going to fear a killer who writes poetry?* As a guy, I'm also pretty sure that it would be completely embarrassing to be murdered and have someone write a corny poem about it.

Regardless of how corny the serial killer's nickname might be, the constant news coverage fueled the fire of fear that engulfed our little town, fanning it into an inferno. If this had happened in New York City, L.A., or Chicago, the news cycle would have already run its course and the parasitic paparazzi would have moved on to their next story. In the sleepy, little, upstate suburb of Westcottville, there wasn't much else to talk about. I hadn't known who Amanda Arseneau was before, but this week her face was burned into my brain from the repeated images we saw on TV and in the newspapers.

As a kid though, I still had that, *it won't happen to me* mindset that we all have until we're about forty. At least I'm guessing that's the age where you get common sense, because that was about the age where my dad stopped being fun. With *The Poetry Killer* still not captured, my parents were as paranoid as everyone else's parents were. They were calling Goob's house to make sure I got there. They wouldn't let me go out unless they could see that I wasn't alone. They forbid me from going into the woods, even if I had friends with me. Of course, none of us obeyed that. That's why I decided to go out that night.

In spite of my parents still being up, I decided to sneak out my bedroom window. After I got out to the backyard, I looped around about three houses, just skirting along the edge of the tree line, before cutting between a couple houses to the street. As usual, there beneath the streetlight, was Bolo. He saw me immediately and cruised over on his board. He stopped and did that move where he flipped his board up and caught it in his hand. I was secretly jealous of his cool nonchalance. The few times I had tried it, I only succeeded in hitting myself in the shins.

"C'mon, let's keep walking," I said. I didn't want to be seen in the street by my parents, so we walked around the corner and slowed a little bit.

"Should we get the other guys?" Bolo asked.

"Nah," I replied. "If they could sneak out, they'd be here already." As we walked, I told him about my encounter in the woods last night. Of course, in my fear yesterday, I was certain that the person I saw in the woods was *The Poetry Killer*. Bolo however didn't spook as easily as I did.

"You know," he said, "it could have been

anyone walking through the woods. You know the older kids hang out there to smoke weed sometimes. I'm pretty sure they're growing it in the back. It could have been one of them."

Before we knew it, Goob and Cliff had joined us. That wasn't surprising. Our parents all often joked that we all shared a single brain anyway. After our first lap around the block, Chuck had seen us and managed to pull his little escape-from-Alcatraz routine to join us. Of course, he decided to hide in the bushes and jump out to scare me to get me back for earlier today. The five of us ambled aimlessly up and down the street, careful to avoid crossing in front of our own homes, as I re-told my story about the shadowy figure in the woods for everyone's benefit.

We debated the merits of abandoning the woods until all this serial killer business was sorted out, but Gooby had a different idea. "We know the woods better than anyone.

Why don't we set the woods up as a trap for the killer? We could catch *The Poetry Killer*!" I kept my mouth shut. Yeah, a bunch of twelve-year-old kids versus an adult psychopath—how could that go wrong? Then to my surprise, Cliff and Bolo jumped on board with the idea.

"Yeah," Cliff said. "I bet that we could handle him easily on our own turf." Then Bolo offered the worst idea ever.

"I saw this movie once where they dug this big pit, put these sharp stakes in it, and covered it with branches. If we did that, *The Poetry Killer* would fall right in, get stabbed, and we'd be heroes for thinking of it!"

"Ummm… yeah, "I offered, "but what if someone who wasn't *The Poetry Killer* fell in?"

Everyone mulled this over for a minute until Bolo finally said, "Guys, I gotta get going. I can feel my sugar getting a little low. I gotta grab a bite to eat." He hopped on his board and glided down the street. In all honesty, as much as I like to portray myself as a rebel for sneaking out at night, I was always nervous about getting caught, so I decided it was time for me to go too.

Of course, when I threw out my excuse for leaving, it was a different story. "I might as well go too," I said. "It's 10:30 and we have a game tomorrow against the Orioles. We can work on our brilliant plan in the dugout." We were at the corner of our street, and I really didn't feel like walking another lap. "See you guys later, don't be a hater," I quipped. As I walked away, I was serenaded by catcalls from the guys and brilliantly pithy comments comparing me to a certain part of a woman's anatomy. That had to be Cliff. He had a gift for language.

As I turned into the backyard, my plan was to do what I had on my way out, but in reverse. I made my way to the very back of the yard on the corner. Normally I'd go right through the little trail at the end of the street, and take the trail in the field that ran parallel with our tree line to avoid being seen lurking in our neighbors' backyards. With *The Poetry Killer* on the loose, I decided to play it safe and stay on this side of the tree line. I was only four houses from mine. I just hoped that a neighbor wouldn't see me, mistake me for the serial killer, and call the cops.

I walked along the tree line with little concern, looking at the fireflies and the moonlight. It really was beautiful out at night, and relaxing too. Ever since I had starting sneaking out at night, I had begun to notice how relaxed I felt when I was alone with the night sounds, enveloped in darkness.

If I didn't have school tomorrow, I would find a spot to sit down and just look at the night sky. As I walked though, I thought I saw a shadow on the other side of the tree line. I stopped, and the shadow stopped. I took two more steps, and the shadow moved with me. The trees and brush appeared too thick for my shadow to show through.

Then it struck me, the moon wasn't behind me. It couldn't be my shadow. "Scooter!" I kind of whisper-shouted. "Is that you?" Then I heard a twig snap. For a split second, I tried to think of what Sonny Crockett would do, but I came up with nothing.

I ran. I ran as fast as I could. I'd love to quote the Flock of Seagulls song that was popular at the time, but at that moment, singing was the furthest thing from my mind. I don't know if I was being followed, but I didn't care. My terror propelled me blindly forward. I was just running. I got to my backyard, turned to the house, leapt upon the table, slid my window up, and clambered in, falling onto the bed. I slid the window closed and locked it. I kept the lights off and stared out that window for probably an hour or more until I succumbed to sleep. Yup, cool as a cucumber. Just like Sonny Crockett would have handled it.

I had fretful, restless dreams of being pursued by a faceless shadow. Each and every time I had that awful, dream-like feeling that I was running as fast as I could, but was still running in slow motion as if I was under water. In the dream, I kept hearing ice-cream truck music, and I was wearing a white linen suit over a teal tank top and loafers. No socks.

Chapter 10

Adults' thoughts and emotions are so rigid that they are often so traumatized by things that they ruminate on them for days, or even weeks. Kids seem to be blessed with short memories and an emotional resilience that adults lack. The next day I barely thought about the incident coming home last night, other than to think that I'll have to be more careful next time, and that it was probably one of the guys or their older brothers screwing with me anyway. I would not put it past Gooby and Cliff to have decided to pretend to stalk me on my way home. Of course, I wouldn't bring it up because if I did, I'd be instantly ridiculed.

On game days, I had very little on my mind other than that day's game anyway. With the serial-killer tension and terror ever present, I think we all sort of latched onto baseball that summer as our mental refuge. I also still had my quest for that first out-of-the-park home run. I wanted it so bad that I daydreamed about that moment almost constantly on game days. I imagined being at the plate and seeing the perfect pitch coming in. I imagined my perfect swing, which I practiced all the time whether I had a bat in my hand or not. I imagined my facial expression as I trotted around the bases. I imagined making sure that I touched every base. I thought about hearing the crowd reaction and of rounding third to see my teammates gathered at home plate to congratulate me.

Chances are that, when it does happen, and I do mean *when*, it will never live up to the fantasy scenario I have in my head. I was probably focusing too much on hitting my home run to the point that my batting average suffered a bit over the last few games. Every swing I made was a home-run swing, regardless of the situation.

We all arrived for the game about thirty minutes early and went through our usual warm-up routines. Andrea and Bolo went out with Coach Thomas to hear the rules and call the coin toss. The rest of us took our spots on the bench.

"Oh my God! Did you guys see _Fridays_ last night?" Cliff exclaimed. "I'm telling you, this show is way funnier than Saturday Night Live. I bet Fridays is going to be on so long that our kids will be watching it. Did you see The Golden Boys skit?"

I hadn't seen it. I didn't want to admit to the guys that even on a Friday, my parents made me go to bed right after Miami Vice. It had, in fact, taken quite a bit of lobbying on my part to get them to let me stay up until eleven pm.

Then Cliff and Goob both shouted in unison, "We're young, we're tough, and we're good-looking!" They almost fell over, they were laughing so hard. Don't you hate when you're left out on a joke?

"I didn't watch it, but I set the VCR," I offered weakly.

"Oh, that's lame," Cliff said. "You're using a VCR?" he snorted derisively. "Betamax is where it's at."

Chuck interrupted, "Hey, guys, I've got an idea..."

Before we took the field for every game, Coach Thomas would have us all gather round. We'd put our hands in together, and one of us would shout a chant everyone would repeat. Usually it was something like, "1-2-3 DEFENSE!" Or it might end with "Yankees" or "Hits!" Today, we had won the coin toss and elected to take the field first. Coach gathered us at the end of the dugout by the third baseline. "Alright guys, and um girl, hands in. Who wants to lead?"

"I got this, Dad," Cliff said. "Alright everybody, on three! One, two, three!" He was joined by the whole team shouting in unison, "*We're young, we're tough, and we're good-looking*!" We all laughed so hard we could barely catch our breath as we ran out to our positions. We even got a little applause from the parents on both sides.

It was another good game for our team. Bolo started pitching and did well, in spite of the fact that Scooter stood behind the other teams' batter making faces and giving Bolo the finger. No one knew why I laughed so much during games. I was really starting to get in the groove at the plate today. I had gotten hits on my first two at bats thanks to Scooter. He would stand by the pitcher and would give me the signs that the pitcher was getting from the catcher. It was like magic knowing what pitch was coming. In truth, it probably didn't matter because even if a good twelve-year-old Little League pitcher intended to throw a fast ball or curve ball, there was probably at best a fifty-

fifty chance any of us could hit the strike zone on purpose. Well, any of us except Cliff. He was nails for us this year. If he was on the mound, we were all pretty sure we were going to win.

Today though, we had Bolo pitching. Bolo wasn't bad, but he'd walk a few batters and give up a couple runs, which still wasn't bad. This game was a tough one though. The other team had jumped out to a 2-0 lead in the first, and we still hadn't scored, despite me being two for two with a double through four innings. In the end, thanks to Andrea and Chuck getting hits in the last inning, we pulled out a 3-2 win to stay undefeated through four games. Thanks to Scooter, it seemed I had my mojo back at the plate as I had three hits and two doubles, but still no home run. For the team though, it was a magical ride so far. Coach Thomas had even offered a pizza and pool party at his house after the season, if we won the championship.

As I packed my bat bag up and prepared to walk home, the invisible-to-everyone-else Scooter appeared next to me. "Cooper," he whispered, as if someone might hear him, "can you come back tonight?" I looked at him and nodded as I slung my bag over my shoulder.

Chapter 11

When I returned home, it was almost the usual, although we did have a family dinner. It was spaghetti Saturday as it always was at our house. It was a mostly silent, tense dinner, but at least the three of us sat together at the table. They didn't ask, but I told them about my game today anyway and was rewarded with a perfunctory "Hmmm…" from my dad. Although, since he was reading the newspaper at the table, I wasn't sure if that was meant for me.

Probably the only way Dad would give me more acknowledgement would be if my Little League team made the Little League World Series in Williamsport, Pennsylvania, and he read about it in the paper. My mom did say, "Well that sounds good, honey. We'll have to make it to one of your games soon."

After finishing my dinner and clearing my plate, I quickly grabbed my glove and told my parents I was meeting the guys at the baseball field for a little more practice. I flew out the door and headed down the street towards the path to the field. Once I crossed into the field, I turned left instead of right and headed for the trail to the woods.

We gathered at our usual spot. Cliff, Goob, and me were there first, followed shortly after by Chuck and Bolo. After a short discussion about today's game and whether or not it looked like Andrea was growing boobs, we got down to the serious business of discussing how we were going to capture *The Poetry Killer*. I gave my little stand-up routine about how embarrassing it would be to be killed and have poetry written about me. They just sat there and looked at me blankly. *One day they'll appreciate my comedic genius*, I thought to myself.

Cliff said, "Umm… ok Coop, is that all you got?"

We spent the next two hours talking and walking through the woods, planning our triumphant capture of the killer who had dared to tread in our territory. That was how we looked at it. We felt like we were protecting our territory. Chances were that the killer might never set foot in the woods. At least that's what I secretly hoped. I was pretty sure I was more afraid of *The Poetry Killer* than he was of a bunch of kids trying to play superhero in the woods. That's when I had an idea that, unfortunately, put me "all in" with this little scheme.

"Hey guys! You know where else we should check out? The cemetery. The body was found there. Maybe that's a place we should be watching, or maybe setting a trap," I offered. "Maybe we'll even find a clue that the police missed." They agreed all around that I had a good idea. The cemetery was just past the west side of the woods and of course, we had a path through the woods that took us to the fence on the side of the cemetery that backed up to the west side of the woods.

We knew exactly where two bars were bent from the fence so that we could squeeze through. That had creeped me out for a few years now. The two fence rungs were bent outward. They were made of steel or iron, and they were bent outward as if someone or something had forcefully broken into or out of the cemetery. It had been left that way for about six years or so. I remember when we first discovered it. The guys just joked about it, but I've always found it deeply disturbing, and now, at dusk, we were sneaking into a cemetery where a murder victim had been discovered recently.

On a Saturday evening, we were pretty sure the cemetery groundskeeper wouldn't be there. Cliff and Chuck slipped through, and then Gooby and I played the "you go first," game for about ten seconds before I gave in and ducked through the opening. Gooby quickly followed, but when I turned to watch Bolo slip into the cemetery with us, I saw him just sort of shuffling nervously on the other side of the fence. 'C'mon, Bolo," I said, "What's the matter?"

He hemmed and hawed a bit and looked down. "I... ummm ... I... uh... don't really like cemeteries," he stammered.

Gooby chipped in, "Don't worry about it, man. Nobody *likes* cemeteries. C'mon, we're all here. It's no big deal."

"Yeah, c'mon, Bolo," Chuck said. "We gotta get this done soon, before it gets dark." I had no idea how scared Bolo must have been of cemeteries to resist all the peer pressure we were bringing to bear upon him.

"C'mon, Bolo," Cliff started in a falsetto, "all your friends are doing it. We'll think you're cool…." Bolo smirked a little at this but didn't budge.

"Nah, guys," he said. "I just can't do it. You guys go on. I'm going to head home. Maybe skateboard a bit. I'll see you later." He put his head down and walked slowly away along the fence, leaving Gooby, Cliff, Chuck, and me watching him as he went.

Bolo

As Bolo reached the baseball field, he walked along, dragging a stick against the outside of the outfield fence. He thought he heard something and glanced at the field. There was no one there, or was there? *Was that a movement in the shadows of the dugout*? he wondered to himself. Dropping the stick he had been making so much noise with, he now kept his eyes glued to the field and dugouts as he walked. *It must have been the shadows playing tricks with my eyes*, he thought as he walked. It was dusk and the sun was setting in the west, making him squint as he looked towards the dugout on the first base side.

When he reached the end of the fence, he decided he wasn't quite ready to go home. *Why bother?* he thought to himself. This was one of those nights where both his brother and dad weren't home. *No need to hurry home to make myself a peanut butter and Fluff sandwich*, he figured. *Maybe I'll just hang out here in the dugout and wait to see if the guys come this way after they're done*, he decided. Bolo ambled down the left field line, kicking third base as he passed, and made his way into the dugout, where he took a seat in the shadows. That's when everything went dark for Bolo.

Chapter 12

In the cemetery, we didn't know where to begin. Chuck suggested we split up and each of us search a quarter of the cemetery, pacing the rows from the outside in until we met in the middle. "Dude, seriously?" Goob said. "How about if we go off in pairs and each search half together. It always worked for Scooby Doo and the gang. C'mon, I'll let you be Fred."

I had to laugh out loud when Chuck said, "I got dibs on Daphne!"

After all our laughter subsided a moment later, I said, "Umm... ok, sure Chuck," followed by more giggling. "Yeah, dibs on a cartoon character. Good luck with that." Besides, I considered myself a little bit more sophisticated, because I thought Velma was attractive in that sexy-librarian kind of way.

Goob and I went to the north side of the cemetery and began in one corner, walking along the fence, while Chuck and Cliff headed to the southern end, beginning in the opposite corner. "What do we do if we find something, just yell?" Gooby asked.

I shrugged my shoulders and said, "I hope we don't find anything worth yelling about." I wasn't too thrilled with this excursion as it was, and I certainly didn't want it getting any more interesting in ways that would probably scare the hell out of me. The low-lying fog that seemed to be forming didn't thrill me either. As long as I could remember, fog had made me uneasy.

"You know what would be really awesome?" Gooby said. "If we had one of those cellular car phones! You know, the one like my mom has in her car. We could call Cliff and Chuck on it if we find anything!"

I laughed. "That's stupid. One, we would need a car and two, the cord would never be long enough for us to walk around the cemetery. They're also way too big to carry around. That whole cellular idea is idiotic. Who wants to carry around a phone all the time? I don't want people calling me wherever I am." We walked along reading tombstones, unaware of the shadow about ten yards behind them that seemed to be silently keeping pace with them.

Cliff

On the other side of the cemetery, Cliff and Chuck were no doubt having a similarly intriguing conversation. "Dude, seriously, you think Andrea likes me?" Chuck asked as they walked along the opposite outer fence looking for anything out of the ordinary.

Cliff chuckled. "Damn Chuck, you are a horn dog. All you ever think about is girls. You'd probably be a way better baseball player if you watched the ball more than you watch Andrea. Hey, are you looking at some of these tombstones? They go back to the 1800s. This is a seriously old cemetery."

Cooper

As we paced the graveyard moving toward the center, we didn't notice that our daylight was dwindling slowly and almost imperceptibly as the sun slipped beneath the tops of the trees. The fog that seemed to be only ankle deep as it slithered into the cemetery twenty minutes ago, had slowly grown in depth as the evening air cooled. Our parents' rule has always been that we have to come in when the streetlights come on in the neighborhood. It was probably that time, but we had no idea because we were too far to see the streetlights.

As darkness fell, the cemetery seemed to take on a life of its own. In the bright sunshine, it was a beautiful, peaceful place, but when you have a twelve-year-old' imagination and you're wading through waist-deep fog and tombstones, the graveyard takes on a feeling in your mind. Much the way that the tendrils of fog seemed to creep into the cemetery as the sun set, the tendrils of fear began to creep into the furthest recesses of my mind, prodding the darkest corners where the arcane creatures of our night terrors hide.

I imagined shadows and movement out of the corner of my eye just about every time I turned around. The crickets' chorus had begun for the evening, and the fireflies were little comfort as I realized it was now dark enough that I could barely read the grave markers.

Then, suddenly, as if I had been on the receiving end of an unexpected punch to the gut, I lost my ability to breathe, or so it seemed. As Gooby and I rounded the end of one row of tombstones, the first stone marker in the next row caught my eye. It was a small, simple stone. There was nothing particularly remarkable about its size or design. It looked new compared with some others. Even in the dimming light, I could see what it said. It was what was engraved upon the stone that startled me. "Nathan 'Scooter' Grottanelli," it read. "Born March 14, 1975 - Died May 19, 1987". Underneath the words, a single baseball was carved.

I hadn't gone to the cemetery for the burial after the funeral, and I hadn't been inside the cemetery in a long, long time. I guess I still thought Scooter was alive because I saw and spoke with him so often. I stopped walking so suddenly that Gooby, who was a step behind, walked into my back. "Hey! Coop, what are you doing?" he exclaimed. I just pointed to the small tombstone. "Hmmm… wow… that is weird," he replied. "I guess I didn't think about where he was buried. So he's been over here this whole time. I wonder if he's a ghost following us around." I didn't laugh. I'm not sure why, but I kind of wanted to hit him.

Instead, I just said, "No, he's not," and resumed walking down the row. I didn't want to stand there contemplating the cold, hard, granite fact that Scooter was really dead.

Then there was a shout from a little ways away. It was Cliff. "Hey guys, come here!"

"Where are you?" I shouted in return. It unnerved me to be shouting in a cemetery. Somehow, it seemed wrong to be this loud. I feared that if there were any ghouls, ghosts, or poetic killers, we would be attracting them with all our noise.

Goob and I met Cliff and Chuck near a small mausoleum in the corner of the cemetery. It was built into a small hill. It was only about seven feet high. It had double doors with what looked like very old, heavy, iron hinges. The door was built into a wide cement façade that made the doors appear to be much more important—more ominous than just any old crypt. The entire façade and doors were covered with a web of vines, which made it appear that it would be impossible to open. Because it was built into the hillside, it was impossible to tell how large it might be inside. The old, wooden door, painted in red paint that had seen better, brighter days, was ajar. Only an inch or so, barely enough to notice, but Cliff had noticed it.

"You guys wanna see what's inside?" he said eagerly. The rest of us eyed each other uncertainly, hands in pockets, shoulders in full "I don't know" shrug mode.

"Umm... ok... I guess so. Why not?" Gooby said.

I wasn't quite so eager. "Well, if it's got a coffin or two inside, what's the big deal? What do you expect to find? It's a cemetery. Besides, I think the streetlights must be on by now, we should probably be going home before we get in trouble."

Chuck just started laughing at me. "Don't be a chicken, Coop!" he cackled. "Whatsa matter? You afraid of a little dead body? I'm in, Cliff, open the door!" Chuck commanded. "Let's see it!"

In spite of everyone else's bravado, I saw more than just my feet shifting nervously as Cliff reached for the door and squeezed his finger into the opening. Maybe it was my imagination, but at that moment, it didn't seem as if the fog was quite as thick, and I thought it appeared as if the ground in front of that mausoleum door was a well-worn path. It was a fleeting thought as my attention was drawn toward the door that Cliff was slowly pulling open. I'd swear he was doing it extra slow to maximize the dramatic tension. The old, brittle vines snapped and gave way. As Cliff gave it a final push and the squeaky hinges surrendered their futile resistance, Cliff let out a bloodcurdling scream, and we all jumped backward. Chuck and I both fell to the ground, turned over, and scrambled a little further away. It was what we heard next that stopped our retreat cold. Cliff had also fallen to the ground, but he was laughing his foolish head off at us.

"Oh my god! You should have seen you guys! You looked terrified! Pussies!"

I got up and tackled Cliff. "You asshole," I said. Chuck joined me a moment later, giving Cliff a charley horse in the thigh before we helped him up. Goob just shook his head at the rest of us and walked over to look into the crypt.

He reached into his pocket and pulled out a little plastic lighter. Since his mom was a smoker, he always grabbed one of her lighters whenever he was going out with the guys. More often than not, it was used for our fireworks, or the occasional campfire in the woods. He thumbed the lighter, and the orange flame sputtered before finally deciding to stay lit. Gooby held it in front of him and extended his arm into the doorway. 'Hey guys, come here. Look at this!" he whispered.

Chapter 13

Bolo

Bolo awoke, or at least he thought he did. He felt dizzy and his head hurt. Then he realized he couldn't really move. He felt his feet bound tightly and his hands tied behind his back. Duct tape covered his mouth, or was it *duck tape*? he wondered. *No one ever says it clearly enough for me to tell.* Unfortunately, Bolo then remembered why he had been thinking about the tape. He was lying on his side on what felt like cold, wet stone. He could feel a large, painful lump on the side of his head. *I hope I haven't bled too much*, he thought. *I wonder how long I've been here.* He remembered walking into the dugout and that was the last thing he could recall.

He squinted into the darkness, trying to ascertain more about his surroundings, but he was having difficulty. His brain felt clouded, foggy. He was starting to get a little nauseous. That was not a good sign. He knew his blood sugar must be getting dangerously low. He needed some food, and he needed it soon. That thought got his pulse racing a little. Bolo knew that if he went too long, he could end up in a diabetic coma or worse. With his dad and brother working evenings, there wasn't anyone home to miss him. *Even when they come home*, he thought, *they might not even check my room. They might just assume I'm in there asleep.* That thought terrified Bolo. No one would miss him until morning.

Bolo rolled and lifted his upper body until he got himself into a sitting position. That made his head feel a little better, but he was cold, wet, and had some kind of tape, possibly named after waterfowl, affixed to his mouth. Then he had a thought more terrifying than a diabetic coma. *What if it's The Poetry Killer?* That thought made Bolo suddenly feel alert as hell, whatever that means. In a panic, Bolo decided he needed to get himself out of there, wherever 'there' was.

From his sitting position, Bolo turned his head and pressed his cheek against what felt like a cinder block wall. He pushed the edge of the tape against the rough cement as hard as he could and then pushed his head forward. It peeled back a little! He repeated, rubbing his face against the rough stone back and forth as hard as his neck muscles could manage. He continued to push, rub, and scrape his face, gaining a fraction of freedom from the tape each time. He could feel a trickle of blood or sweat or both, start to trickle down his chin. *Damn, that's gonna leave a mark*, he thought to himself. He didn't know if his blood-sugar level was making him delirious. He hoped he had more time. Then he remembered how coyotes will chew their own arm off to escape. He hoped it wouldn't come to that, but he decided that if he had to do that to escape *The Poetry Killer,* he would.

Chapter 14

Cooper

We scrambled to our feet, and pushed and pulled at each other all the way over to the mausoleum doorway as we jostled for position. Gooby's arm was outstretched with the lighter in his fist just inside the doorway, illuminating the interior enough for us to see that there was absolutely nothing to be afraid of. It was empty. No coffins, bodies, or drawers. Cliff said to Goob, "Give me the lighter." None of us were sure what Cliff had in mind, but Gooby handed the lighter over. Cliff took it and walked right inside. It only appeared to be about eight feet by two feet inside. As Cliff took a few steps in, he said, "Oh my God, you guys. You are not going to believe this." We all leaned in a little closer. Cliff whispered, "Wait, I'm not sure… let me look a little closer." We all shuffled a step or two into the mausoleum, when, suddenly, Cliff jumped and let out a bloodcurdling scream, as if he'd had a limb severed.

We all jumped and ran backward a few steps, hesitating, unsure if we should run for our lives or try to save our friend from whatever evil monstrosity that might have been hiding in the dark abyss at the back of the crypt. That's when Cliff started laughing again in that annoying cackle of his. The three of us rushed into the crypt and tackled him on the floor, giving him the best noogies we could manage in such a confined space, while he continued to laugh and mock us as "chickens". *Oh my God*, I thought. *Cliff is such an ass*. That thought was cut short and replaced in a heartbeat by terror.

Cliff had dropped the lighter, plunging us all into darkness. The door slammed behind us, and we heard the latch lock. I heard a whoosh and a thunk of metal forcefully hitting cement. Chuck tried to stand up, but quickly hit his head and fell back on top of the pile of us. I could feel the panic in me and in everyone else. My heart raced and my breathing was fast and came in jagged gasps. From the sounds around me, I wasn't the only one. Gooby was screaming and trying to claw his way over us as he tried to climb over the pile to get to the door.

"STOP!" I shouted. 'Nobody move! We need to calm down. And figure this out. Screaming isn't going to help. Cliff, can you light the lighter again?"

I heard a sigh from my right. "I can't find it. I dropped it when you guys tackled me. Why don't we feel around?" After a few seconds of scuffling, Chuck said, "I got it!" We all heard, Click, click. Click, click. "Shit, it won't work. I think it's broken. Clank! "Ow! My head!" Chuck exclaimed.

I hesitantly and fearfully reached up, to feel what seemed to be metal stakes that had shot like spears out of openings about four feet up the wall. Had any of us been standing, we would have been impaled. As it was, we were now imprisoned in the inky darkness. Caged like rats that had walked into a trap where someone had simply pulled the stick out, allowing the box to fall to the ground.

"Hey guys!" Cliff shouted. "There's a wheel or crank of some kind over here." From the direction of his voice, he sounded like he was at the end opposite the door.

"Dude, seriously," Gooby said, "do you really think you need to yell? We're all like three feet from you." Chuck laughed at that, and I did my best to stifle a snort. *Typical*, I thought to myself. *Nothing stops us from making fun of each other. I hope that changes as we get older.*

"Well, turn it then," I said. "It can't hurt." I heard Cliff give a grunt.

"It won't turn. I think it's rusted," Cliff said. In spite of what must be cooling air outside after sunset, it felt like it was getting warm in the crypt. I silently said a little prayer that this thing wasn't airtight. Cliff let out another grunt of exertion and exclaimed, "It's moving a little. It felt rusted shut, but I think it's starting to turn!" We could hear a creak and a groan of metal, as well as what might have been flakes of rust falling to the floor. "I think… it's starting… to... give," Cliff said through gritted teeth. It sounded like he was putting all of his strength into it. I hoped it that it would open the door, but feared that it could trigger something worse. We had already dodged a bullet, or rather, lethal metal spikes. Who knew what other traps this tomb might hold for us? I hoped it wouldn't become our tomb as well.

It was getting downright hot in here. I didn't feel short of breath, but the smell of our sweat was starting to fill the air. That and the smell of the cherry cough drops

Cliff was always sucking on. He had terrible seasonal allergies, and the menthol in the cough drops helped open his sinuses. At least I hoped sweat and cough drops was all the others smelled. I had indulged in a milkshake earlier in the day, and I could sense my body was about to remind me of its intolerance for lactose. I was fearful of what might happen if Cliff got that crank wheel to turn, but I was more fearful of what might happen if he didn't.

Gooby was on the verge of hyperventilating. I could hear his rapid breathing next to me. He didn't think anyone knew about his claustrophobia. I did. I had been around him enough that I had noticed the subtle signs of anxiety whenever we were in situations where space was limited. It was always especially bad when it was somewhere that was confined and dark. I don't know why he was so scared of small places, but I never said anything to him about it because he was the only one of the guys that had never called me Super Pooper Cooper over and over. I knew he was on the verge of a major freak out, so I did the only thing I could to distract him and everyone else. I let one rip. There's nothing like breaking wind to break the tension. This one was definitely not silent, but it might have been deadly.

"Oh my God Cooper! Ugh! That is awful! What is wrong with you?" Chuck said. "Cliff, get us out of here quick before we all suffocate." I could hear Cliff laughing, and I could also sense a little relief from Gooby next to me. I could hear him smile a little. Yes, I said *hear* him smile. You know how you can hear a smile in someone's voice. I heard a smile in Gooby's voice as he laughed with the rest of them at my digestive misfortune. He sounded genuinely relieved for a moment.

"Super Pooper Cooper strikes again!" Cliff said as he laughed. "And I thought the dead bodies were going to smell bad!" he chortled.

Suddenly, we heard a loud snapping and a creaking, groaning sound, as the last of the rust gave way and what sound like metal straining against some tremendous force. In the dark, we couldn't see anything, but we could feel, and we felt the cold, damp, cement floor of the crypt vibrate and start to shift beneath us.

Chapter 14

Bolo

Bolo spit the last of the tape from his mouth and exhaled. He slumped against the wall, exhausted from his struggles to get the tape off his mouth. His cheek was scraped and bleeding, but at least his mouth was free. He didn't even consider yelling for help. This didn't seem like the kind of place anyone could hear him from. He also didn't want to alert his captor to the fact that he was in the process of freeing himself.

Bolo rarely, if ever, counted on or asked anyone for help. When his mom had left the family without a word, he was left with a hole in his heart, and in his trust in others, that might never be filled. At least he didn't think he would ever trust or rely on another person. *If you can't trust your own Mom*, he thought, *then there's no one you can trust.* Sure, his dad and brother were there in his life every day, but every day, they also left him home alone from the time he got home from school until the time he put himself to bed, or more often, until he fell asleep on the couch watching television.

From the time he was nine, his dad and brother had both worked the evening shift. He had to come home to an empty house and take care of himself. He thought that his dad and brother were probably as shell-shocked by his mom leaving as he was, so he just sort of decided that he had to suck it up emotionally and deal with it like they were. He knew his dad was a good man. His dad kept groceries in the house and made sure Bolo had everything he needed to take care of himself after school, including checking his own blood sugar and taking his insulin or a snack, whichever he needed. Bolo didn't know any different. He just assumed that was how people learned to grow up. He had always been self-reliant and being knocked out and imprisoned wasn't going to change that, so he went back to work.

Bolo had seen a magic show on television once where this really funny guy uncovered the secrets to all the magic tricks you always see. He acted like he was some serious bad ass by defying the "Magician's Code" and revealing how tricks were done. Bolo remembered a move he did where he showed a Houdini escape from a box, but for the show, the box had been made of Plexiglas so you could see what went on inside. The magician had been gagged, and had his hands handcuffed behind him and his feet shackled before he was locked inside the clear box.

What Bolo remembered specifically about this particular escape trick was that the magician had been able to take his cuffed hands from behind him and slide them down the back of his legs. Then with a little bit of a strain, and what looked like a painful stretch, he was finally able to pull his bound hands beneath and over his feet to bring them in front of him, where he used a tiny key he had in his mouth to unlock them. Bolo thought that if he could get his hands in front of him, he could then chew the duct tape off his wrists, and he'd be free.

Bolo was thankful that he had a bit more room to maneuver than the magician did. He allowed himself to fall over onto his side on the floor. The floor was cold and damp, and he could feel the dampness soaking through his clothes. As he began to shimmy his arms down behind him, his face rubbed on the floor, and his scraped cheek stung like hell. He ignored it and before long, was trying to stretch his arms behind him as far as he could. *God this hurts*, he thought to himself. He thought it more as a fact than an emotional declaration. To Bolo, life was difficult one way or another all the time. It was just how things were. He didn't think that anybody really lived like *The Cosby Show*, where the kids were polite and the parents compassionate and wise. Life was hard. Bolo never expected anything more.

He could feel it. He could feel his shoulders and surrounding muscles stretching. The edge of the tape around his wrists was starting to get past his heel. He thought he was going to make it. He wriggled and shimmied on the floor, angling and arching his back, trying desperately to squeeze another quarter inch of slack from either his body or the tape. He was starting to feel too dizzy to go on. With his teeth gritted, he pulled as hard as he could and felt two things at once. One was the tape finally sliding free past his feet, and the other was a painful pop in his left shoulder as it dislocated.

Holy shit! That hurts like hell, he thought to himself. He lay there for a few minutes, waiting for the pain to subside, suddenly appreciating the cool dampness of the floor against his sweaty and bloodied face. He tried to focus and gather his thoughts. It was difficult because his brain wanted to drift, to dream. *No. No, no, no!* he shouted at himself inside his head. He had never gone this long without food or insulin. He was in trouble, and he knew it.

Chapter 15

Cooper

As the crank wheel gave one last cracking sound and spun free in Cliff's hands, the floor dropped out from under us. Or rather, one end of the floor dropped out. With a loud thunk noise, the far end of the floor where Cliff had been cranking the wheel just dropped. Cliff hung onto the wheel for dear life. His feet hung down as Chuck and

Gooby tumbled by and into the darkness. As I slid downward, I was in a sitting position with my feet in front of me. I was trying futilely to backpedal. My fingers grasped for purchase on the cold, damp floor and found none. The incline was too steep and slick for me to resist the force of gravity. In the darkness, I felt Cliff's legs and feet drag over me as he hung from the handle. At the last moment, I reached back over my shoulder. I took a stab in the dark and managed to clutch the very bottom hem of Cliff's jeans in my fingertips.

In a panic, Cliff started kicking, but I had gotten my other hand there and clung to his leg like my life depended on it, which for all I knew, it did. "Cliff, stop kicking," I shouted.

"You idiot," he shouted back. "I can't hold on. My fingers are slipping. Let go!" There was no way in hell I was letting go. Clinging to Cliff's legs would either save me, or we would fall to our deaths together. Apparently, it was going to be the latter as Cliff's twelve-year-old fingers quickly tired of the task of supporting two people. His hands slipped off the crank wheel and we both fell into the darkness, screaming our crazy heads off the whole way.

We didn't talk much as we fell to what we assumed would be our immediate death. Most of our conversation on the way down consisted of witty repartee such as "Oof," and "Ugh!" Occasionally, I threw in an "Oww!" just for good measure. Cliff, very creatively, decided to add in, "Ow, ow, ow," to punctuate each time that some part of his body contacted a hard surface as we tumbled down what felt like a slippery, stone slide. We tumbled painfully for what seemed like an inordinate amount of time, all the while trying to stop ourselves with our feet or hands, but the incline was too steep. Occasionally, I would roll into and over Cliff and, in a matter of moments, he would return the favor. We tumbled so long in the darkness that I became disoriented and dizzy. I had no idea when or if I was upright or upside down at any given moment.

We tumbled out onto a flat surface that was as cold and hard as the tunnel we had just fallen out of. We landed in a heap, and we both just lay there for at least a full minute, sucking in deep, cool breaths from… well, from wherever we were. I took a brief inventory of my body. I felt out of breath, bumped, and bruised from head to toe, but it didn't feel like I had broken anything. "Cliff, you ok?" I asked.

With a slight groan, he muttered, "What do you think, shithead? I swear, if you ripped my new Jordache jeans, I'm going to kill you when we get out of here." I have no idea why Cliff liked Jordache so much. Personally, I thought the embroidered pockets were too gaudy. I was a Calvin Klein man myself. At least I thought of myself as a 'Calvin Klein man'. The lack of commercial endorsement offers coming from the Calvin Klein Company indicated that I was probably alone with that thought.

I pushed myself up to the sitting position and immediately felt blood begin to drip from my nose. I quickly reached down and pulled the bottom of my shirt up to my face to try to stop the bleeding. Lying back down, I waited.

As I lay prone on the floor, I could hear Cliff getting up to his feet. There was still no light in the room, if it was a room, but Cliff slowly shuffled his way forward with his arms stretched out in front of him. "Wud are you doing?" I asked, my speech impaired by the pressure I was putting on my nose.

"I'm trying to find a wall and then hopefully a door," he replied. "Where do you think Goob and Chuck are?" Cliff asked.

"I hope they're not dead," I replied.

It was odd that they hadn't ended up the same place we had, I thought as I lay there wondering if the bloody nose was some sort of hemorrhage caused by a blow to the head during our fall down here. Yeah, I was a bit of a high-strung hypochondriac. Whenever I had something physically wrong with me, I always assumed the worst. Every headache, in my mind, was definitely a tumor until proven otherwise.

"Well, they fell before us," Cliff speculated, "maybe they found a way out when they got here. Hey, here's a wall. I'm going to feel my way around until I find a light switch or door or something." I heard some scuffling. "We're definitely in some kind of underground cavern or something. These aren't regular walls. They feel like they're just dug or cut out of the ground," Cliff said.

Suddenly, there was flash of stupendously bright light. I shielded my eyes with my arm. "There we go!" Cliff said. I sat up and slowly pulled my arm away from my eyes and squinted as my eyes adjusted to the light. Once I became accustomed to it, I realized it wasn't very bright. Cliff stood by a doorway-sized opening in what did indeed appear to be a sort of cave hewn out of rock and earth. There were a few rotting beams running up the walls and across the ceiling, but most of the exposed wall and ceiling was rock and dirt. One small, bare, musty, yellowed bulb swayed and flickered as it hung from the rafter above me. 'Dank' might be the one word best prepared to describe where we found ourselves. I couldn't fathom why a room like this existed.

"Sonofabitch! You did rip my jeans!" Cliff exclaimed, his voice echoing around the cave and down the dark tunnel.

"Oh, screw you!" I fired back. "Those are way too tight for you anyway." Cliff always seemed a little too fashion conscious for a twelve-year-old guy. I was pretty sure that his older sisters were dressing him like he was their own life-sized Ken doll.

"Well, do you think we should go down there?" he asked, pointing his arm into the inky dark tunnel. Based on my extensive experience watching the horror movies that we sneaked into at the drive-in, I was pretty sure that the answer to 'should we go in there' should always be no. If I was watching the movie of Cliff and me right now, I know there would be ominous music and everyone watching would be yelling at the screen, "No! Don't go in there!" Of course, we couldn't hear the ominous music, so I sat up, clambered to my feet, and walked over to Cliff. For a moment, we both leaned forward and peered into the darkness of the tunnel. It looked like an extension of the "room" we were in. It also kind of reminded me of one of those mine shafts you always saw in old western movies, the kind that usually collapsed on people.

"Gooby! Chuck!" I shouted, making sure that any nearby serial killers could more easily pinpoint our location. My voice seemed to have been swallowed up and smothered by the darkness. Where I had expected an echo, there was nothing but deafening silence. I'm sure it was my pre-teen imagination running wild, but I swear I could feel a malevolence emanating from the blackness in front of us. It felt like a pull, almost as if the inky void emitted a gravity that was trying to drag us into it. The feeling was more than a feeling of physical gravity as well. I felt a chill run up my spine and goose bumps rose all over me. I saw Cliff wrap his arms around himself and rub his skin a little, as if he were cold.

"Well, here goes nothing," Cliff said with a cheeriness that belied his fear. He was always our leader when things got tough. We each had our moments, but most consistently, when we needed a decision made, Cliff took the reins and said, "Follow me." Usually, we did because we didn't have any better ideas and because at twelve, we didn't want to be called chicken in any situation.

I don't think it mattered that we decided to go forward. I don't think we had a choice. The force that I felt seemed to be pulling at our souls. It felt dark and unyielding, like a magnet pulling at my mind and my heart. I knew we couldn't go back up the long, slippery slope we had tumbled down, but I desperately wished we didn't have to go forward. It just felt… wrong in some way that I couldn't define. As much as my mind tried to resist, when I looked down, I saw my feet moving forward of their own volition. I was a passenger trapped in my own body. I could see Cliff ahead of me walking forward as well. I wondered if he felt like I did.

We walked forward, not speaking, almost in lockstep. That feeling of wrongness grew inside me. I observed that the tunnel seemed to slope slightly downward as we walked. I was nervous, worried about going deeper into the Earth beneath a cemetery, but it didn't appear I had a choice. We trudged onward in silence until after what I estimated in my mind to be the length of a football field had elapsed. I saw light ahead. It appeared to be an opening to a larger area. The light appeared to be of the fluorescent variety and was flickering as if there were shorts in all the wiring. That's the way it looked. The way it felt to me was despair. I'm not sure what it was, but I was suddenly overwhelmed by such a sense of hopelessness that I didn't feel as if I could go on. I also felt as if I couldn't resist either. It was as if my soul was being sucked out of me little by little, with every step closer to that room with the flickering lights. I had that passenger-in-my-own-body feeling again, and felt tears begin to run down my face in hot, salty streams. I didn't know why. I wanted to scream out loud, but I couldn't. My body just kept carrying me forward.

Chapter 16

Chuck

Gooby and Chuck landed in a heap with an audible thud. They had endured a similarly painful downward journey as Cliff and I had, but they had ended up in a different cavern somewhere else beneath the cemetery. At least, they thought they were still beneath the cemetery.

"Chuck, are you alright?" Gooby asked.

"Well, I seem to still have all my limbs. How about you?"

Gooby snorted. "I'd be better if I wasn't underground in a cemetery." He shook himself and took mental inventory of his body. Everything seemed sore and scraped, but intact.

Chuck did the same, although his ankle felt sprained. "Shit, I think I hurt my ankle." He tried to stand,

"Ow, ow, ow!" he exclaimed. The ankle was too painful to support him much. "Shit, how am I ever going to get back up there?"

Gooby grinned and said, "Hey, don't worry about it. I'll leave you here, find my way out, and then send help for you. Don't worry, Chuck. I'm sure the C.H.U.Ds will take good care of you." His laughter at his own joked echoed around the cavern.

Chuck picked up a handful of mud and threw it at the sound of Gooby's voice. "There is no such thing as C.H.U.Ds!" Chuck practically shouted.

Gooby laughed again. "Well, if there are, we're in the right place to find them." He paused. "Or for them to find us!" Raucous laughter and the sounds of Chuck blindly try to wrestle Gooby to the ground filled the chamber.

Gooby had intentionally brought up C.H.U.Ds. He knew it was one of Chuck's buttons. About six months ago, we had all watched the movie C.H.U.D. on cable one night when we were hanging out at Cliff's house. It was a cheesy horror movie starring Daniel Stern. The acronym C.H.U.D. stood for Cannibalistic Humanoid Underground Dwellers. Most of us thought it was an awesomely cool and unintentionally funny movie. Not Chuck. For some reason, it freaked him right out. We didn't notice it when we were watching the movie, but we noticed that after watching it, Chuck never went home after dark unless someone walked with him. In a conversation he later regretted, he had, in a moment of weakness, admitted to us that he worried that there really could be C.H.U.Ds.

Like the empathetic and sensitive twelve-year-old kids that we were, we never let him forget it. We were a creative bunch and there were a few hilarious practical jokes that we still laugh about to this day. Let's just say that the combination of Cliff's old Freddy Krueger costume, and Chuck having a first-floor bedroom, was not a fortuitous situation for him.

"Wait. Shhhhh! Listen," Chuck said. "What is that?"

"It sounds like music," Gooby replied. "Where could it be coming from down here?" A pleasant, singsong type of tune seemed to fill the chamber. "C'mon," Gooby said, "let's find out where it's coming from. It might be our way out." They climbed to their feet, but Chuck had to have Goob's help to pull him up. Once upright, they were able to get a better sense of where the music was coming from.

"Wait, let's move slowly over to a wall and then feel our way along to where the door must be," Chuck suggested. His ankle hurt like hell, and he didn't want to lean on Gooby anymore than he had to.

Shuffling slowly together, they quickly found a wall. It felt like a wall in an underground cavern. It was cut from rock and dirt with the occasional rotting, wooden beam that must have originally been placed there for support. The stone and dirt walls were cold and damp, with rivulets of water snaking their way to the floor here and there. Gooby took the lead as they shuffled along slowly, keeping a hand to the wall. They were dirty and sore, and the wall offered much needed support. They paused to rest. Chuck hadn't realized how much the fall down the tunnel had taken out of him. When they first landed, the adrenaline from the terrifying fall had heightened their alertness. Now that they weren't flailing for their lives and had a moment to pause, they realized how tired they felt, sleepy even. "C'mon Chuck, we can't stay here," Gooby mumbled.

They resumed their shuffle along what started to feel like a round room. The lilting, almost carnival-like melody was still filling the air. If anything, it felt louder they thought. *Felt?* Gooby thought to himself. *Yes, felt*, he decided. He could feel the music as if it was swelling up from within his own chest and filling his brain, almost pushing out all other thoughts. *It seemed to have a magnetism to it*, he thought, *a mental pull*. His mind was drawn forward, towards it. It's like he was feeling an invisible string from the center of his chest, pulling him onward.

Chuck was feeling similarly, but his ankle kept reminding him he had sprained it. At least, he hoped it was only a sprain. He didn't want to miss much of the baseball season. At the same time as he thought this, he shoved that thought aside. He didn't want to stop listening to the music. He wanted to walk towards it. He gritted his teeth through the pain in his ankle and concentrated on letting the music soothe him from within. As he focused on the music and its healing properties, he began to feel a numbness, or lack of feeling, in the ankle that had pained him so much only minutes earlier. *Was it minutes?* he thought to himself. He wasn't sure. Time must be passing, but like your fingertips trying to grasp a single ice cube, just barely out of reach, the idea kept slipping away, and he couldn't quite focus his mind enough to guess, or even sense, the passage of time. The music seemed to fill his mind, sweeping everything away. Nothing else seemed important. Nothing except following that song to its source.

They reached the door together. There was an old, brass knob that had seen better days. The wooden surface felt rough, and rotted. *Like everything down here*, Gooby briefly thought before the music again soothed his worries. *There's nothing to worry about*, he thought, as long as they could get to the music. The song seemed to be speaking to them. Gooby just knew that if he turned this knob, he would only find goodness and light. Happiness was inside that song and even though there weren't words, that pleasant, child-like song was telling him that he would be safe if he just followed it. As if in a dream, Gooby saw his hand reach out and turn the knob. The door seemed to swing wide open before them, almost as if they had been expected.

Chapter 17

Bolo

Bolo awoke to find himself lying on the cold, damp, rough floor of a different room than he recalled having been in before he passed out. He still felt groggy and nauseous, but the rest his bout of unconsciousness had forced upon him helped focus his mind. The room he was in appeared to be a classroom, kind of. The fluorescent lights flickered dimly, almost giving a strobe-light effect to the room.

He was lying on the floor between rows of school desks that had seen better days. They were the kind that had the desktop attached to the chair by the arm. There were roughly a dozen of them in various states of antiquity and disrepair, arranged into three rows. Chillingly, he also noticed a set of handcuffs attached to the leg of each desk. The one nearest to him appeared to have dried blood on the edges of the loose end of the cuff. He looked down to see that there was indeed a handcuff attached to his ankle, but the other end was free. He didn't have any recollection of how he had gotten into this room, nor did he remember falling to his current position. Judging from the broken, rusty leg of the overturned desk next to him, he surmised that he had struggled to free himself, breaking the desks leg and falling over. He must have lost consciousness from the combination of his exertion and his likely low blood sugar.

Bolo lifted himself up to a sitting position carefully as his head swam. He didn't know if it was due to his blood sugar, if he had been struck, or if he had hit his head when he fell. His eyes adjusted to the light, such as it was, and his vision cleared as he focused on the nearest wall. What he saw there drew his attention, and he carefully pulled himself up, first to a kneeling position. His head started to swim again, and he could feel a painful throbbing in his brain. Bolo took a deep breath and focused his mind. He knew these were all symptoms of low blood sugar, but something else felt off too. Something that was hard to put a finger on.

He gathered his thoughts again, sharpening his focus as his doctor had taught him to do when he felt woozy. He pulled himself to standing, leaning heavily upon the desk nearest him. He stood for a moment to catch his breath again, and make sure he wasn't going to pass out. The wall was only about six feet away. He thought he could reach it in just a few steps. He stood there staring at the wall for a minute, trying to comprehend what he thought he saw under the flickering fluorescent lights. These didn't seem to be normal fluorescent lights. They looked normal, but the constant flickering and the gray dinginess of the light they gave off seemed to suck the life out of the room. There didn't seem to be any real color anywhere. The effect of this was draining Bolo mentally and emotionally.

He cautiously took a first step, and then another, just sort of sliding his feet about a foot forward at a time. He began to sway and held his hands out, as if he were walking a tightrope. He focused his mind, and gritted his teeth in concentration, as he took two more steps and reached the wall, arms outstretched, supporting him. The effort had been exhausting.

Once he caught his breath and gathered his thoughts, Bolo again looked closer at what he thought he had seen from where he had been earlier. It was exactly what he thought it was. Cubbies. A whole bunch of cubbies just like along the wall of almost every elementary school classroom in the world. They were wooden and four rows high. The bottom of each cubby was labeled. At first Bolo thought there were initials at the bottom of each cubby, and there were, kind of.

As Bolo stood there contemplating the pattern, he counted the cubbies. Twenty-six exactly. Four rows—the top two rows having six cubbies each, and the bottom two had seven. His eyes scanned each row. When he was done carefully looking at the little label at the bottom of each cubby, he looked again just to make sure. *Yup*, he thought to himself, *this just got seriously creepy.*

The tiny pieces of yellowed paper affixed to the bottom of each cubby with clear adhesive tape were aged and curling. Each one had just two letters on it, and the two letters were the same. Bolo looked at the rows and sequences again just to be sure. AA, BB, CC…it went on until on the bottom of the last cubby, he saw ZZ. It was the alphabet. *What could this mean?* he wondered. He looked within each cubby and several of them had a small, single item inside, while others had nothing. He reached into the first cubby—AA it was labeled. He found a lanyard, like those commonly worn around the neck to carry keys. Imprinted upon it in gold lettering was "H.C.E.S."

Bolo pondered this for a minute. His mind felt something vaguely familiar, but just out of his mental grasp. He was exhausted and his blood sugar was likely very low. It was taking a conscious effort just to stay upright and focused. His left hand grasped the edge of one cubby, supporting him. He likely would slump to the ground without it. He knew he couldn't last much longer without rest and food. As he stood there visually scanning the cubbies, he saw something that made his spirits soar.

There within cubby LL was a candy bar, still in the wrapper. It was a kind you could still get in stores, but the wrapper looked different. It looked somewhat dated. *But who cares?* he thought to himself. Bolo reached in, grabbed it, and immediately tore away the wrapper. He didn't even pause to inspect it before he greedily gobbled it down. He didn't care how old it might be. If he died of a diabetic coma, it wouldn't matter if he got food poisoning. It may have been his imagination, but he felt better almost immediately. His mood and energy soared. *Thank God*, he exclaimed in his head. Then two things happened in quick succession. The music started, his legs gave out, and he collapsed to the floor. As he was falling, he clutched desperately to the lettered cubbies, trying to fight off the effects of gravity… but gravity wasn't taking no for an answer. During his fall and just before passing out, when his head hit the floor, he noticed that the bandana he usually had tied around his thigh was resting in the cubby labeled RR.

Chapter 18

Gooby

Gooby and Chuck couldn't believe their eyes. In fact, just like people that over act in sitcoms, they actually rubbed their eyes and looked again. As the music continued to play in their heads, they gazed in wonder at the world before them. Without realizing it, they were going down the steps into the brightly colored panorama.

It was as if someone had re-created the magical candy wonderland from that movie. There were trees made of giant candy canes and the grass appeared to be the same kind that filled Easter baskets every year. There were chocolate mushrooms here and there and jellybeans strewn about the ground like pebbles. *What was that movie?* Gooby thought to himself. As the music continued to pull on that thread in his mind, his feet kept walking deeper into that kaleidoscope of colors, smells, and sensations, until Gooby's next thought was, *Movie? Why was I thinking of a movie?* He began to sway with the music as he drifted more than walked down the path.

Chuck

Chuck had rushed headlong into the room and immediately crouched down to greedily scoop handfuls of liquid heaven into his parched mouth from the babbling brook of chocolate milk. He could not get enough of the delicious, life-sustaining liquid. He had no other thoughts than to drink and to fill himself until he was satiated, and he didn't feel like that would happen anytime soon. He suddenly had a fearful thought as Gooby began to wander in his direction. *What if he wants to steal my chocolate river? What if he wants it all for himself?* Chuck continued to gulp it hungrily down, ignoring the signals that his stomach was urgently sending to his brain. That part of his brain had long ago shut the door and hidden itself in a dark corner. *Kill him*, Chuck thought. *That's what I'll do. I'll kill him if I have to. If he tries to steal my chocolate drink, I'll have to kill him. It's mine.* As these thoughts ran through his mind in an endless loop, he kept one eye on Gooby and lowered his head to slurp directly from the flowing river of chocolate.

Gooby

As Gooby drifted, observing his new surroundings with wonder, he noticed that absolutely everything seemed edible—deliciously, delectably edible. As he strolled, he noticed mounds of red, shoelace licorice lying here and there. He loved shoelace licorice, especially red. His dad liked the black licorice, but Gooby always thought he was crazy. Nobody liked black licorice.

Gooby sat on the ground beneath two piles of the stringy, sugary delicacy, picked up one string of the red licorice, and slurped it into his mouth, then another and another. He thought that he could just live here forever, even if all he had to eat was red, shoelace licorice candy. One after another, he put it into his mouth. Some he slurped and swallowed whole, while others he chewed up. After a while, he got creative, tied some into knots, and ground them into a little pulp between his molars before swallowing the mouthful.

Chuck continued to drink as if he had walked into that room straight from the surface of the sun. He had forgotten about the possible threat of Gooby stealing from his chocolate-milk river, and Gooby had forgotten everything but the song and the delicious, red, shoelace licorice. A short distance from Chuck, Gooby had lain upon his back and covered his body with the piles of red licorice. The music continued to play on as Gooby sighed to himself and decided he had found heaven. He was finding ever more creative ways to eat the licorice, and decided that as long as he didn't run out of it, he had no reason to get up from this spot.

Chapter 19

Cooper

I still have conscious thought, I thought to myself, *but it's slipping away. I know who I am, but I don't know how Cliff and I got here, or why his jeans are ripped from the cuff up to the knee. Am I a zombie, or maybe a C.H.U.D.?* I wondered as I observed my feet trudging forward with me onboard as a helpless passenger. *I don't want to be a zombie. I hate eating uncooked meat.*

I felt like I was on an escalator. In my mind, I was standing still, afraid to go forward towards that room with the weird, flickering light within. Every time I looked around through eyes I no longer felt in control of, I could see and feel my body moving. That invisible string attached to my chest had a hold on me as if it were a fish hook, and I was being reeled in.

Cliff was being reeled in too. Absent were his usual quips and bravado. He looked as helpless as I did. The open door was waiting for us, calling to us, inviting us, only it didn't feel like an invitation. I heard a crash within, as if some chairs had suddenly been overturned. I was fearful and terrified because, against my wishes, my body was taking me towards that noise instead of away from it. Tears streamed down my face, but I kept walking, as did Cliff. We were almost there. In a moment, I would see what had made those noises. *Would it be the last thing I see?*

As Cliff and I stepped inside the room, the scene inside was not what I expected. The shock somehow broke the magnetic hold upon both of us. There, lying on the ground in front of us, was Bolo, apparently unconscious, with his face scraped and bleeding. His clothes were wet and torn. One of his sneakers was missing, and his bare foot was bleeding. He looked like hell.

The room, which looked like it had been roughly carved out of the dirt and rock, had the same rotting wooden beams we had seen elsewhere. This room however, appeared to be a rough approximation of a classroom. By the flickering light of poorly maintained fluorescents, the kind that you find in institutional-type places, a floor of cracked paving stones had been put down. Actually, I doubt that the lights were originally flickering, nor was the floor probably cracked when it was first put down, but years of ground water leaking into and out of the walls and ceiling had taken a toll on... on... whatever this was supposed to be. I don't know what it was supposed to be, but I knew what it was—creepy with a capital C.

There were several aged, wooden desks in rows, except for the two that were overturned. On the leg of each desk was handcuff so rusty it looked like it would give you tetanus if you were chained with it too long. On the right wall, where Bolo was laying on the floor, was a group of crudely made cubbies. The scene was so bizarre, it was dizzying to me.

Cliff seemed to regain his bearings a little better and a little quicker than I did, and rushed over to where Bolo lay on the ground. "Bolo, Bolo! Wake up." I could see that Bolo was still breathing. As Cliff shook his shoulders, gently trying to rouse him, I noticed the broken, rusty handcuff still attached to his ankle and the Charleston Chew wrapper still clutched in his hand. It's funny how you notice little details like that in the midst of a crisis, isn't it? Then I remembered his diabetes, and I hoped he was doing ok.

I let go of the breath I had been unconsciously holding when Bolo's eyes opened. "There you go," Cliff said. "This is no place to take a nap." Bolo shook his head to try to clear the grogginess and accepted Cliff's help moving to a sitting position, leaning against the cubbies.

I knelt down next to him. "Dude, you alright? What happened? How did you get down here?" Bolo exhaled and took a deep breath, still trying to clear his head.

"Did you just call me dude?" he said weakly. I smiled. If Bolo was with it enough to mock me, then he was going to be all right. "Oh my God, you guys," he exclaimed. "You have no idea how weird this is." Cliff and I looked at each other as if to say, *Yeah, I think we do have an idea how weird this is*. As we would soon discover though, we didn't have any idea how weird it was going to get. "We have to get out of here!" Bolo continued with a look of terror in his eyes.

"Dude, just relax,' I said as I patted him on the shoulder. "We're going to be out of here soon," I lied. I had no idea how we were going to get out of there. S*hit, I said it again. I have to stop saying dude,* I thought to myself.

That was a good question, I thought. How do we get out of here? I could see another entrance, or perhaps exit, from the 'classroom' we were in, but justifiably, I was afraid of going further and deeper underground. Nothing good had happened so far, and I was pretty sure that going farther wasn't going to help matters any.

Then Cliff chimed in. "We have to find Goob and Chuck."

In my mind, I thought, *The hell we do! Let's just get out of here and send the cops in after them*, but what my mouth said was, "Yeah, where could they be?" Mentally, I was kicking myself for not suggesting that we run for our lives, but I knew Cliff was right. We couldn't leave without Gooby and Chuck. They wouldn't leave us either, and if we were to run into the killer down here, it would be better to have more of us. Hopefully, that wouldn't happen because. Physically, none of us were feeling like we were ready for a fight.

"Well, there are only two directions we can go," Cliff said, "and we know they aren't where we came from, so I guess we have to go through there." He pointed towards the tunnel on the other side of the room. Bolo was unable to remember how he had come to be in this room, so he didn't know what might lay ahead down that tunnel. We helped him to his feet. The sugar from the candy bar seemed to be having a restorative effect upon him. His face wasn't quite so pale and his eyes looked clearer and more focused. "Well," I said with a shrug of my shoulders, "we might as well see what we can find." I grabbed his bandana from the cubby and shoved it into my pocket as we turned toward the tunnel. As I walked away, something clicked in my mind. Bolo's bandana was in the cubby marked RR.

With that, the three of us shuffled slowly towards the entrance to the next tunnel. "Coop, grab the back of my jeans, and Bolo, you grab his. We have to stay together in the dark," Cliff instructed. Bolo and I didn't have any better ideas, so we followed his lead. Like kids at daycare holding onto one of those ropes with the loop handles, we proceeded in a line, shuffling along, one hand on each other and one on the wall.

We hadn't heard it when we were in the 'classroom' but as soon as all three of us were in the dark tunnel we could hear it—music. It was a pleasant melody, which evoked thoughts and feelings of happiness. I couldn't quite put a name to it, but some little kernel somewhere in my mind recognized it from my childhood. Thoughts of bright summer days and cones full of soft-serve ice cream filled my head. It was almost as if the music was telling me to follow it to where that sunshine and ice cream-filled world might be. From the feel of my hand on the waist of his jeans, Cliff felt as if he must be swaying in time with the same song. A different kernel of consciousness somewhere else way back in my mind was trying to sound an alarm to me, but it felt so far away that I didn't want to listen.

I felt a tug at the back of my jeans. It was Bolo. He whispered urgently at me, "Cooper! Look back. Look back at the door." Because he was still fighting against the effects of his low blood sugar, Bolo was concentrating on keeping his mind focused just as a matter of survival. Unlike Cliff and me, he was still focused on our surroundings. He didn't seem to be hypnotized by the song the way we were. I looked back like he said I should, and my blood suddenly ran cold. The doorway or entrance to the tunnel was gone. We had only traveled a very short distance down the tunnel, and if that room was lit, we should still be able to see it. It was gone. It has been replaced by an inky blackness that was as deep and impenetrable as the void of space.

I jerked on the back of Cliff's jeans to rouse him from the spell. At first, he didn't respond. He kept walking forward, and Bolo joined me in trying to pull him backward. The floor was wet and slippery, and we were losing the battle. I never realized how strong Cliff's legs were. He was, in fits and starts, pulling both Bolo and I forward. "Cliff! Stop it!" I shouted. Nothing. It seemed as if his legs continued to drive forward with renewed vigor.

The song, as pleasant as it seemed, was rising to a crescendo. Damn, it was familiar, but I couldn't figure it out. As it got louder, it seemed to be becoming distorted. I'm not sure if Cliff was growling as his knees continued to churn forward, but he sure looked like it as his bared, gritted teeth joined a vacant look of ferocity on his face.

Bolo let go and quickly moved ahead of Cliff. He tried to brace his feet behind himself and with his hands on Cliff's shoulders, he leaned forward into him. With me pulling on the back, we were able to slow his progress, but he still seemed entranced by the song, which grew louder with every step we had taken forward.

As loud as it was, it didn't seem to be coming from any specific location. It seemed to be coming from within my head. Bolo and I were shouting at each other, but we couldn't hear what we were saying. I could see Bolo gesturing to me, but I couldn't get the gist. It was crazy. Then as I watched, dumbfounded, Bolo reared back and slapped Cliff hard across the face. It must have been a hell of a slap, because I could hear it over the music in my head as Cliff's head snapped sharply to the right. *Um, yeah, that'll leave a mark*, I thought to myself.

The slap seemed to have the effect Bolo had hoped for, as I felt Cliff stop trying to walk forward. He shook his head and looked at both of us. "Did you just slap me?" he said, as he rubbed his jaw. As crazy as the situation was a moment ago, I still had to turn away and stifle a laugh when I saw the bright red handprint on Cliff's face. If we get out of here alive, we'll probably be laughing about that for a few days. In my head, I had to correct myself. *When* we get out of here, I thought.

We tried plugging our ears but the song wouldn't go away. I could still feel that pull on my soul. We communicated with each other by gesture. Whatever force was trying to pull us forward, was obviously not cognizant of the fact that we were walking the direction it wanted us to anyway. We couldn't go back the way we came. It appeared to have just disappeared, as if it had blinked out of existence the moment we stepped out of the "classroom". The only way out, and possibly the only way to find our friends, was to go forward into whatever it was that wanted us.

The bright light at the end of the tunnel grew brighter and larger as we walked. It appeared to be a round opening. We kept looking each other in the eyes to check in and make sure that we were still "there". I had to make a conscious effort to focus my mind on the simple act of walking and looking at my friends. My mind kept feeling that pull, that desire to dream. I had that feeling I get when I'm kind of falling asleep, and I'm all dreamy and not certain if what I perceive is real or a dream. Then, if Bolo or Cliff would get my attention with a snap or a nudge, I had that exact same feeling you do when you dream you're falling, and you awake as if you had been shocked or something. It was jarring, but I was glad to be pulled back to reality. I had no desire to let that pull drag me under again, because I didn't know if I'd ever come back.

When we finally reached the opening, I took a deep breath of relief. I felt as if my sanity had been hanging on by a thread as we walked that last fifty yards. Then Cliff screamed. Not a word or exclamation—just a scream of terror. There, in a large cavern like the others we had seen and been in, were our two friends, Gooby and Chuck.

Cliff's scream made them both freeze and, in that moment, my mind took a snapshot I will never forget. Crouched over on all fours with his elbows in the mud, Chuck was drinking mouthful after mouthful from a gulley of flowing, muddy water that started in the side of the cavern and flowed across the floor, before disappearing into a crevasse. His face was covered in mud and the front of his shirt was brown and soaked through to his skin. To his right, Gooby was laying on his back, with a half-chewed mouthful of worms—big, fat night crawlers. I started retching at about the same time he did, as he dropped the two handfuls of mud and worms, and rolled over and started vomiting violently.

After everyone had stopped puking, we looked around the cavern. There was an oil lamp in the corner, providing just enough dim illumination to leave the outer edges of the room in shadow. Chuck and Gooby had no recollection of how they had gotten into the cave, nor of anyone else having been there to light the lamp. Cliff, Bolo, and I each related our perception of the hypnotic trances we had been in. When Gooby and Chuck related their stories, one detail was eerily similar. The music. We had all heard music, but none of us could remember exactly what it was.

Bolo had heard the music, but described it as seeming far more distant in his mind. His guess was that because of his low blood sugar, he had been making a concentrated effort to stay focused and conscious. As a result, he was less susceptible to the trance-inducing effects of the music, or whatever it was that seemed to be kind of broadcast down here. "This is the first time I've ever been glad to be diabetic," he said.

With a smirk, I quipped, "If your blood sugar is low, do you think eating worms would help?"

"Asshole," Gooby said as he punched me in the arm.

"What? Too soon?" I laughed. My ribs hurt when I laughed. I hope I hadn't broken any.

As we explored the cavern, we found a small opening on the other side. We looked in and could see that it opened into a large tunnel that we could at least make our way through on hands and knees. The opening was barely large enough for someone to slip through on their belly, but that's what we decided to do. We didn't want to go back where we had been, and we didn't think we'd be able to get out that way. We all agreed that if the tunnel didn't descend, we would see where it went. Chuck grabbed the lamp.

The tunnel appeared to go on for quite a ways, but after scampering like monkeys for just thirty feet or so, we found a door. A perfectly ordinary looking door, except that it was only about three feet high. It was wooden with a shiny handle. "Well, shall we go in?" Cliff asked.

I don't know why he said 'shall'. *This hardly seems like the time to be pretentious*, I thought to myself.

The door appeared to open outward. Cliff tried the knob. It turned, but the door didn't budge. He put his shoulder into it, only to hear a creak, but the door stood firm. "Let me try it," Chuck volunteered. He grabbed the knob, turned, and slammed his shoulder into it as hard as he could. A creak only slightly louder than Cliff's had elicited came from the door.

"Ok, how about if we all throw our weight against it at the same time?" I suggested. Everyone looked around and shrugged their shoulders, as if to say, why not? At this point, we all looked weary, bedraggled, and covered in mud. I know I didn't want to go another step in any direction.

"One... two... three!" Cliff shouted and at once, we all threw our weight against the door. It creaked, and then cracked. "One more time! One ...two ...three!" Cliff commanded. We again attacked the door, as if we were just one big, human bowling ball. As our shoulders and weight barreled into the little door, there was no resistance as it was pulled open from the other side, and we all went tumbling out into the darkness.

This time however, there was no free fall into the depths of the Earth. We landed on regular old dirt and slightly dewy grass. As we disentangled ourselves, rolled over, and looked up, we saw that we had come barreling out of the crypt we had entered in the cemetery. Then we all screamed and crab-walked backwards a few feet. If I were an adult, I would have literally had a heart attack.

Standing there, holding the door to the crypt open, was *Genzler*. In kind of an odd monotone, he said, "You kids really shouldn't be out here at night. It's not safe." It was the first time I had ever heard him talk. It was kind of creepy. His face was blank and expressionless. He just stood there as if he was waiting for some sort of response from us.

"Umm... yeah, you're right," I said. "We should go." I looked at the others, and we all looked at each other, pausing, not sure what to do. I got up slowly, brushing off as much of the dirt as I could. The others did the same.

"Uh… thanks *Genz*... err... Greg," I said and began to turn away. The others followed my lead. When we reached the southwest corner of the cemetery, we all hopped the fence. I risked a look back in the direction of the crypt, and I could see Genzler there just as we had left him, staring placidly at us. Even at this distance, his creepy stare gave me the shivers and I couldn't wait until we were out of his sight.

We didn't talk much as we walked home. Our bodies and minds felt too weary to do much other than trudge as far as our houses. I couldn't wait to fall asleep. That's all I could think of, just rest. I needed rest more than I had ever needed it. I was so tired that I could barely climb in my window. Slipping in quietly, I stealthily pulled the window closed, making sure I locked it behind me. I slipped out of my filthy clothes and into my pjs, lying on my bed. My lids grew heavy immediately. I didn't try to fight off sleep. I just let it overtake me as if it were a wave pushing me down, forcing me under with its weight. I don't recall dreaming, but the last thought I had as I slipped into darkness was a song. A happy singsong tune playing in my mind.

Chapter 20

I awoke the next morning, not with a spring in my step, but with a sore body and a very fuzzy recollection of a nightmare. The longer I was awake, the more slippery those memories became. I lay in bed trying to remember. *Trying to remember what?* I thought to myself. With the sun streaming through my window, as if this was going to be a spectacular summer day, I rolled over and happened to glance at my desk, spying my baseball glove. I sat bolt upright. *Yes!* I shouted in my mind. I scrambled out of bed and looked at the clock. Butterflies began their delightful dance in my stomach. I felt as if it were Christmas morning.

Once our baseball season had got going, it became pretty obvious after about two weeks who the good teams and the bad teams were. My team, the Mullane Motors Yankees, was one of the good teams this year. In fact, we were undefeated so far. We all had dreams of making All-Stars and going to the Little League World series. It definitely looked like Cliff and I were on track to make All-Stars. I was hitting .532 and Cliff was pitching like Nolan Ryan. A few of our other teammates were doing well too, but were no locks for All Stars. As well as I was playing though, I still didn't have my home run.

That's why today felt like Christmas. We were playing the Griff's Septic Tank Repair Orioles. It was an unfortunate sponsorship pairing this year because the team really did stink. They hadn't won a game all season. I did feel badly for the couple of guys I knew on the team, but I didn't feel so badly that I wasn't dreaming of hitting my first ever out-of-the-park home run against them.

I quickly got dressed in my uniform and ran to the kitchen to grab a quick breakfast. We had the nine am game today. I didn't mind because it meant that we got to use the field before the chalk lines were all messed up. I loved that, because when you had the first game and those bright, white chalk lines were still perfect, it almost looked as good as a major league field. Inhaling a bowl of cereal and a swig of juice, I ran to my room to get my equipment. "Don't wear your cleats in the house!" Mom shouted after me. Geez! Just one time I forget to take my cleats off on the hardwood floor, and she'd never let me forget it.

I didn't even ask if she and Dad were going to the game. By now I knew the answer, or answers, I guess would be more accurate. It didn't matter that I had stuck my Little League schedule to the fridge. Mom was either going to be at "Aunt Shirley's house checking on her" or she had to "go grocery shopping". Dad, of course, was either golfing with his work buddies, or had a project he was working on that required his full attention.

I stopped to sit on the step and tie my cleats. I could see Cliff and his dad already walking down the street to go to the field. I ran to catch up with them. "Hey," I said. It was our usual greeting.

"So Cooper," Cliff's dad interrupted, "you think you're up for starting the game today?"

"Umm... well, yeah," I began to reply, a little confused. "Don't I always start?"

"No, no, I mean start as in pitching," he added. I hadn't started any games yet this year. Typically, he let Cliff pitch the first three or four innings and then pieced together the last couple innings with the rest of us. He had used me in mop-up duty here and there, but starting was a whole other deal in my mind. It was pressure. It was giving up the first run. It meant setting the tone for your team for the game.

"Uh... sure, I'll pitch," I stammered.

We lost the coin toss and our team had to bat first. I was still batting clean-up, fourth in the order. When I came up to bat, I was still preoccupied with worry about my pitching. I dug in my feet and looked to the mound. There was Scooter, clowning around the pitcher. He was literally dancing around the mound like a lunatic. I was so busy trying to stifle a laugh that I wasn't ready for the first pitch and got a strike called on me. Putting my hand up, I signaled for time and stepped out of the box. I looked over to the third-base coach to get the signal and to take a deep breath. The way I was hitting, the signal was always the same, swing away.

I stepped back in and this time, I gave Scooter an angry glare to say, *Stop distracting me*, but I think the pitcher thought I was trying to stare him down. With the next pitch, he hit me right in my ass. Not that I had much of one, but his accuracy was uncanny. I tossed my bat aside and jogged to first as the ghost of Scooter accompanied me, rubbing his ghostly ass, and miming that he was crying.

After the first half of the inning ended, it was my turn to pitch. My first pitch was a wild one that went over the head of the catcher. Fortunately, it was the first pitch and no one was on base, but it sure didn't set a good tone. I could see my fielders fidgeting nervously. My next pitch was a ball, but then on the third, I finally got a strike. Unfortunately, my pitching wasn't as good as my hitting. It wasn't pretty but I managed to get out of the inning with just one run given up.

I wasn't up to bat next inning, so Cliff and I stepped behind the dugout so I could throw a few practice pitches. Much to our surprise, we found Chuck and Andrea back there, swinging their bats and talking. Cliff and I looked slyly at each other but didn't say anything; although, I'm sure Chuck must have noticed our smirks. *Good for Chuck*, I thought to myself. We were at that awkward age where we weren't sure what to do with girls. On the one hand, we kind of liked them, but on the other hand, when we did like a girl, we just got nervous and teased her because we didn't know what to say. To see Chuck making a little headway with a girl, put me to shame. Cliff and I talked a good game, but neither of us had really had a girlfriend yet. If Chuck beat us to the punch on that one, we'd have to tease him mercilessly.

In my second at bat, I managed a weak grounder with eyes that got me to first. Because of how bad their pitching was, I was having trouble hitting. They threw so slow that my timing was off. The players on the team, who shall remain nameless, who weren't as good as I was, were having a field day hitting because they were finally facing pitching they could handle well. I was frustrated, but it was all right. We were winning 6-2 heading into the final inning, and my pitching hadn't been too bad.

I had one more at bat. My last chance today to try for a home run against pitching that would barely be passable two levels beneath us. I walked to the batter's box and dug in. I didn't even look at the third-base coach. I didn't care what the situation was, or even about the outs or if there was anyone on third. This ball was going out. That's all there was to it. I was ready for each pitch, but each of the first three were way out of the strike zone. I'd look like an idiot if I even tried to reach them with my bat. Ghostly Scooter was leading off second. This was it. I couldn't let him walk me. If the next pitch was even in the same zip code as the strike zone, I was going to take a hack at it.

The pitcher released the ball, and it seemed to trundle leisurely towards home plate. I had to remind myself to wait a split second longer for the slow pitch. It was going to be high and outside, but I thought I could reach it. I watched and waited. Patience, and then controlled fury, like I had been taught. I saw the ball coming in and it looked good enough. I felt something click in my mind and from above my right shoulder, my bat sliced through the air in a smooth, powerful arc towards the strike zone. The barrel of the bat, the fat part, caught that ball dead center. A round bat hitting a round ball just perfectly at the one spot that mattered. *This was it*, I thought to myself as I cockily tossed my bat aside and started to jog to first.

I watched the ball as I was running. I also saw the outfielder. At first, he just shuffled his feet as he watched the airborne ball heading his way. Then came the part I always loved. You see the outfielder watching the flight of the ball, tracking it, when all of a sudden, his eyes get big at the moment he realizes that the ball is gonna keep going. This outfielder did that and as I rounded first, I saw him get that "Uh-oh" look in his eyes. He turned away from the infield and ran towards the centerfield fence. I triumphantly threw my arms in the air! My first home run. *Yes!* was my only thought. I heard the gasp of anticipation from the parents watching. Then, as I reached second base, I saw the outfielder jump in the air at the fence. It was only a four-foot high outfield fence and my ball just cleared it. The outfielder's arm cleared it too and he pulled the ball back in with the very end of his outstretched glove. It was what the highlight announcers always called a sno-cone grab. "Awww!" was the vocalization from our side of the field, while the other dugout was filled with raucous cheers. I threw my head back and let my arms fall to my sides as I slowed to a walk and headed back to the dugout.

The game was over and I had gotten plenty of "Nice game" pats on the back, but I couldn't smile. My dream had been right there, and I literally watched it get snatched away. Everyone was celebrating our undefeated record as they enjoyed the after-game snack. In spite of myself, I lightened up a bit and joined in on the banter. Bolo had noticed that Chuck and Andrea were sitting side by side on the bench, and nodded in their direction to get my attention. Goob noticed too. We wouldn't publicly embarrass Chuck, but he was in for it the next time the guys were hanging out together.

That night at about 9:30, I slipped out of my back window and into the shadows. I skulked through the backyards until I reached the trail that would take me to the field. As I approached the field, I saw Scooter their playing catch with himself by throwing a ball up in the air and then running under it to catch it. When I reached the fence, I sort of shout-whispered, "Scooter!"

He turned his head. The ball dropped to the ground behind him and just disappeared, leaving a little wisp of vapor where it had been. As I crossed the line and walked over to where he stood at his usual shortstop position, I shook my head, laughing. "It's a ghost baseball and you still missed it. How does that happen?"

He scowled at me. "Yeah, very funny. Nice home-run trot today." I mimed pushing him, or tried to push him, but of course, my hands had no effect on him.

Are ghosts allowed to be sarcastic? I wondered. Wasn't there some ghost code of conduct he had to abide by? I'm pretty sure that making fun of me wasn't going to help him get his wings or move on to the afterlife any sooner.

We walked along the outfield fence from pole to pole, and then down the line, all the way to home plate. Scooter still couldn't leave the field with the exception of the dugout. "So why are you still here? I asked. "I mean, why haven't you gone to heaven or something?"

"I don't know," he replied, either out loud or in my mind. I still wasn't sure. "I feel like I have to do something.

I'm not sure what it is, but I feel like there's something kind of holding me back from being free." We walked in silence for a few seconds.

"Did you forget to feed the dog or something? Cuz if you did, I could just go over and give him a few treats or something," I said with a smirk. This time he tried to push me, but all I felt was a little cold breeze on my shoulder where he touched me.

"Scooter, if I tell you something, will you promise not to think I'm crazy?"

He shook his head at me and smiled. "Dude, you're already sneaking out of your house at night to play baseball with a ghost. Why would I think you're crazy?" He had a good point. By now, nothing seemed too far-fetched.

"Ok, last night something weird happened to us over in the cemetery, but I'm not sure what it was." I paused to gather my thoughts into something coherent as we kept walking. A low-lying fog was settling in on the dewy grass around our ankles, or at least my ankles. When it was foggy, I lost parts of Scooter in the fog. I never said anything because I didn't want to embarrass him. "Last night, did you see anything weird over at the cemetery?"

Scooter shrugged his shoulders. "I'm sorry, Cooper. I can't see the cemetery. What happened?"

I had to sigh for a second before I pushed myself to go on with the crazy story. "Me, Goob, Cliff, and Chuck decided to snoop around the cemetery to see if we could find any clues to the little girl's killer." I shouldn't have paused. I knew Scooter wasn't going to miss an opening.

"Hmmm... let's see," he said. "Nighttime, cemetery, looking for a killer. Gee, how could that go wrong?" He laughed, but I wasn't in a laughing mood.

"Shut up, you idiot. You didn't have this much to say when you were alive. *Now* you're Mr. Chatterbox?"

Scooter stopped laughing and looked down as we walked past the dugout. If it was possible, I think I might have been the first person to ever make a ghost feel bad. Now I felt like a jerk. "So anyway, we found this crypt open, and we decided to take a look inside."

He stopped and looked at me. "You know I'm biting my invisible tongue right now, right?"

"Yes, I know we were stupid to try this, but something really weird happened. Although, I can't remember what it was. I know we went into the crypt and the door got locked behind us, then we fell down a tunnel, and that's the last thing I really remember." We stopped, with him standing on first base. He actually was taller when he did that. *How does a ghost stand on something*? I wondered. Was he just trying to be taller than me because I had hit puberty and had grown an inch since he died?

"So you don't remember what happened after that? Up until when?" he asked.

"I don't know!" I exclaimed. "That's what I'm trying to say. We all went into the crypt and something happened down there. When we got out, Bolo was with us and *Genzler* was there.

"Wait! What? *Genzler* was there? In the cemetery? At night?" he exclaimed. "Wow, that is creepy!"

"Yeah, and it seemed like a lot of time had passed, but when I got home, it was like five minutes after I left. I had weird dreams all night too. And then that jerk robbed me of my home run today. The even weirder part is that no one mentioned it today. It's like it never happened."

"So no one else said anything?" he asked incredulously.

"Yeah, I know. Right? None of them have even come close to hitting one out this year!" Scooter laughed and mimed knocking my hat off my head.

We continued to walk and talk, discussing our possible theories about what might be going on in or beneath our neighborhood. Then Scooter surprised me by saying, "How're things going with your folks?"

I snorted derisively. "Who?" I replied.

"Your parents," he said again.

"Who?" I repeated.

"Oh... I get it," Scooter said. "That bad, huh?" I guess maybe it wasn't that bad. Unlike Bolo, I did have parents to come home to, sort of. I didn't usually have to make my own dinner anyway. "Is your dad still drinking?" Scooter asked. "You know we all know. It's alright. You don't have to be embarrassed. It's not your fault. We just never said anything because, well, we didn't know what to say. But you know what? All our parents have issues. I'm not going to say anything about the other guys. That's for them to say, but you might be surprised. If I'm not around to talk to, the guys would understand. You should try them out sometime."

We kept walking around the bases, but we were quiet for a few minutes as I thought about Scooter's advice. That was funny to think about—getting advice from Scooter. In a million years when he was alive, I never would have considered asking him, of all people, for advice. I guess dying really forces you to mature a bit. What a crazy summer it was. I was glad I had Scooter to talk to, even though the fact that I was talking to the ghost of my dead friend might mean that I'm crazy, the conversations always made me feel better.

Chapter 21

I awoke leisurely, the way I did on most Sundays, just sort of lying in bed, dozing on and off, thinking of what I would do with a beautiful summer day. It was Sunday and I had absolutely no plans or obligations. The mid-morning sun was beaming into my room through the curtains and illuminating my Miami Vice poster. It was the cool one where Crockett and Tubbs were standing in front of that white Ferrari Testarossa that they always drove around.

I could hear the sounds of the suburbs on a summer day. A couple of neighbors had already started mowing their lawns. I could hear the young children riding their bikes and playing outside, without a care in the world. Dogs barked happily, or at least I interpreted their tone to be happy. Who the hell knows? They may be wagging their tails sarcastically for all we know.

I rolled onto my side to look at the clock. 9:51 am. *That seems alright*, I thought to myself. *I guess I could get up and see what they guys are doing.* Then I noticed something odd on the floor near to the laundry hamper by my closet. A bandana—a red one in fact, just like... wait a minute... just like Bolo wears tied around the leg of his jeans. *Hmm... what is that doing here?* I wondered, but I knew that I knew. I didn't know how or why it was here, but I had that feeling you have when you know that you know something. It was that feeling when you know the information is stored somewhere deep within your brain, but you can't quite reach it with your mental tongs.

I rummaged about my brain for a full thirty seconds before my mental tongs got distracted by my rumbling stomach and latched onto the memory of chocolate chip waffles in the freezer. That got me going. I sprung out of bed and dressed quickly. There was no need to shower because I knew I'd be in someone's swimming pool, probably by lunchtime. After wolfing down a quick but substantial breakfast, I headed out the door. Goob and Cliff were in Cliff's driveway playing basketball, and I joined them.

Cliff was a naturally fluid athlete. Goob and me? Not so much. It was more like he was playing basketball while Gooby and I were trying to see how much abuse the rim could withstand, although truth be told, one of us had a harder time finding the rim. Before long, Chuck ambled over to take a few shots with us and, shortly thereafter, Bolo cruised up on his skateboard. That was how it usually went. We never really communicated anything ahead of time; we just sort of assembled in one place or another. It was almost like we were drawn to each other. I'd like to believe we had some sort of special psychic bond, but it was more likely that we all just knew that on any given day, at least one other of our friends would be somewhere outside looking for company.

This was how almost every other perfect summer day began. We would just walk out of our houses and find each other. The day stretched out ahead of us with unlimited possibilities and no time pressure whatsoever. Whatever we did, we did it at a leisurely pace that most adults would never recognize. After shooting baskets for a little while, we ended up walking around the neighborhood, going for that walk that had become so familiar to us. It was kind of our group therapy, I guess.

Then suddenly and without warning, we all registered various states of shock when we passed the Genzler house and there was Greg Genzler standing on the driveway at the front corner of the house, holding a broom and staring at us. "Holy shit!" Cliff muttered under his breath to me. "I don't know why, but that guy gets fucking creepier every time I see him." We always found his staring creepy, but for some reason, this time it brought a chill to my bones. Unconsciously, I literally crossed my arms over my chest defensively and hugged myself, as if I were cold as we walked by. As we kept walking, I risked a glance back to see if he was still staring at us. He was and maybe my mind was playing tricks on me, but I could have sworn that *Genzler* gave me a tiny, almost imperceptible nod. I looked away and quickened my pace a bit to move to the front of our little group.

After a swim and some peanut butter and marshmallow sandwiches that were generously provided by Cliff's mom, we headed out to the woods. They were brighter today than usual. The brilliant, midday summer sunlight filtering through the high branches warmed the air in the shade a little more than usual. We walked our paths and checked on our fort. It wasn't really much of a "fort" in the traditional sense of the word, but for some reason, whenever we built any kind of structure on our own, we always called it a "fort."

It was maybe eight foot by eight foot and about six feet high. We had built it with some two-by-fours and pieces of plywood we had scrounged from the half-built houses that were under construction on the other side of the woods. I suppose some might call it stealing, but in our minds, if you just left something outdoors lying around, then you obviously didn't care too much about it. Let me tell you though, as a twelve-year-old boy it is not easy sneaking a four-foot-by-eight-foot piece of plywood anywhere by yourself. We had built the fort back in the middle of a group of bushes and shrubs near the old well. Then we covered it in pine tree boughs to hide it from view. We were proud of our camouflage job. If you didn't know where it was, you probably weren't going to find it.

The old well wasn't a well like you see in fairy tales. It was just a hole in the ground about two-and-a-half feet across and about twelve-feet deep. It was lined by what looked like cobblestones. We assumed that at some time in the distant past it probably was a well for some pioneer farmer. It always seemed to be filled with dank, murky water, from where, we didn't know. It was a well, but I was pretty sure that no one would ever be throwing coins in there wishing for anything. We had thrown plenty of stuff in there over the years, never to see it again.

We knew the depth of the well because one day we had "borrowed" some rope and a measuring tape. We had tied a ten-pound dumbbell to the end of the rope and lowered it until it hit bottom, and then we measured the rope. The rope, dumbbell, and measuring tape never made their way back to our homes. I'm sure it drove our dads crazy thinking that they kept misplacing stuff.

We loved our fort though. We completely thought we were such bad asses with our secret hideout. We would sit in there and plot our imaginary battles against the invading hordes that we fantasized might come from the nearest neighborhood. We didn't know who those kids were or if they even gave a rat's ass about us, but we imagined that because we had such an awesome little world with our woods and our fort that they, of course, would want to come here and take it over from us.

We had brought a couple of old chairs out there that we had scavenged from the curb on garbage day. On the rusty, little card table in the middle of the tiny room was an old deck of cards that were faded and curled from the moisture they'd absorbed out there. We were forever trying to think of a way to get electricity in the fort, but in the end, we were stuck with just flashlights. We had a little stone-lined pit in front of the fort where we had our campfires, and would roast marshmallows and cook hot dogs on a stick. As far as having your own place at twelve, we thought this place was the shit.

Today as we walked our usual loop of our trails in the woods. Chuck was telling us about some spy movie he had seen recently and wanted to show us how in the movie they had managed a gunfight while zip lining between skyscrapers. I don't know what he thought he was doing. I couldn't understand how he thought he was going to zip line one-handed, while miming that he was shooting at us. I tried to explain my thoughts on this subject but Chuck just responded by calling me a name that brought female genitalia to mind. "Ok, but when you're dead or paralyzed, I promise that I will stand over your dead body and say 'I told you so'," I shouted to him as he climbed the tree.

We looked up into the canopy of branches as Chuck climbed the tree the twenty-five feet or so to where the zip line was tied. He paused for a moment to unhook the handle and get himself situated. I watched nervously as he wrapped one arm over and around the zip-line handle. That just didn't look doable to me. As much as I liked being right, I admitted to myself that I really didn't want to see Chuck fall to his death. I was rooting for a fall and just a sprained ankle though.

Then, with no evidence of fear, Chuck leapt from the tree with his arm crooked around the handle. Because he was hanging by one arm, he was off balance and swung awkwardly as he began to slide. For a moment, I caught my breath as the rope line dipped under his weight. He was at the zip lines highest point now and if he fell from there, it would surely be to his death. The rope held, and as he stopped swaying and began to pick up speed, he turned to us and held his fingers out like a gun, miming his thumb moving up and down as if he were pulling a trigger. "Now!" Cliff shouted and Bolo, Goob, and I took our hands out from behind us and began to pepper Chuck with a barrage of pinecones as he flew down the line.

I didn't know if Chuck planned to drop off the line or try to bounce off the tree at the end, but it became a moot point when Bolo wound up and hurled a pinecone at him. It was one of those really big ones that you'd fill with peanut butter and suet and hang from a tree in your yard for the birds in the winter. Bolo didn't pitch for our Little League team, but you know the saying, "Even a blind squirrel finds a nut every now and then." Unfortunately for Chuck, Bolo had picked a bad time to find his nut, or rather, Chuck's nut.

At first, we began to laugh hysterically when we saw the pinecone hit Chuck directly in the groin. Then, as Chuck reflexively released his grip on the caster-wheeled handle, our laughter suddenly stopped. We saw his arms begin to flail as if he was on the end of a diving board and losing his balance. Sadly though, he wasn't on the end of anything, and the ground was rushing up to meet him at an alarming rate of speed.

The fates and fortune were kind to Chuck as he hit the downslope of a dirt mogul and slid into a muddy bowl at the bottom. "Thanks, you jerks!" he shouted at us. He got up and paused, bent over, to catch his breath. His back was scraped and covered with mud, but otherwise, he seemed none the worse for wear. When he had caught his breath, he stood up quickly and flung handfuls of mud at us, as if he were a primate defending his territory. Our laughter renewed again, when we could tell that he was really all right. We each took a couple turns on the zip line, but no one tried it one-handed, and we refrained from further hijinks involving projectiles. Cliff, of course, said he hadn't thrown any because he was saving his arm for pitching the day after tomorrow. Then, just like in the movies, there was a rustling in the trees and several birds took flight. We all looked around at each other. Cliff gave the shush sign, as if it was necessary. A couple of us slowly crouched down and picked up rocks.

The woods had grown eerily still. Cliff broke the silence. "C'mon you guys! We know you're out there. We heard you!" There was no response. Nothing. There were no birds chirping, and no rodents scampering. The woods seemed pregnant with an eerie silence that hung in the air as we looked around. This time there was no raucous laughter. Chuck motioned for us to circle up. We did. We arranged ourselves in a circle with our backs to each other so we had eyes in every direction. We waited. After about one minute of silence, I looked around at everyone as if to say, *C'mon, isn't this enough?* Goob and Chuck both shook their heads at me. Then two more minutes passed without another sound. It was as if the woods suddenly became a vacuum or a black hole.

The sun even seemed afraid as it hid behind a cloud, leaving the woods cool and dark again, as if evil had suddenly swept through like a winter wind. Cliff motioned for us to follow. This time there would be no screaming dash for home. This time, apparently, we were going to stay and defend our territory, no matter whom or what might be out there. Still in our protective circle, we moved as a group slowly down the trail towards our fort. If we were going to take a stand, it was going to be there.

As we reached our fort, we picked up all manner of implements. We had a couple of shovels, a hammer, and a saw. Unfortunately, we had left our baseball bats home today. We expanded our circle to encompass our fort. Although we put on a brave front, I would guess that all the guys were as scared as I was. Hopefully, it wasn't evident in my face. I could feel the tension in my brow as we heard another round of rustling in the brush. This time, it sounded closer. There didn't seem to be any animal noises like growls or grunts, but there weren't exactly any human noises either, just that rustling in the bushes that seemed to be getting closer. It wasn't like in the movies where some kind of giant beast was rampaging through a forest, casually pushing trees aside. To me, it sounded more like something bigger than a squirrel or rabbit, but definitely not a bear, I hoped. I felt myself gulp a little.

"It's over here!" Cliff suddenly shouted as he heard some branches moving.

"No," Gooby exclaimed as he heard a rustling in the bushes nearest him, "it's on my side!" I was between the two and, from the sound of it, I thought it was coming right at me.

"No," I shouted. "I've got it!" My breathing was rapid and shallow as I held the shovel straight out in front of me as if I were preparing to joust. The cool breeze that had come when the sun disappeared seemed to be kicking up pine needles and the dry, dusty dirt on the floor of the woods. I shuffled back and forth, first a step or two to the right, and then I quickly adjusted and moved to the left, as the sound seemed to move that way. I risked a glance around, and the other guys seemed to be experiencing the same thing I was. We all looked terrified, which was fine with me because that's the way I was feeling. It seemed as if we were in the middle of some sort of maelstrom. I imagined that this must be what it is like being in the eye of a tornado. The wind was kicking up, and I couldn't tell if the brush was being rustled by some creature within or just the wind. What the hell was going on?

The wind seemed to be increasing in intensity and volume, as if a jet engine were mere feet away from us. It was crazy. Then over the roar of the wind, I heard it. A note. Just one note. I think the other guys heard it to because we all glanced back and forth at each other with a horrified look of recognition. Then the first note was followed by another and another. In spite of the roar of the wind, it was apparent that we were all hearing it. It was like we were in the eye of a tornado all of a sudden. The only thing missing was Miss Gulch riding by on her bike. What was perplexing was the music. We were all hearing it, but not over the music. We were hearing it inside our heads.

We all maintained our positions, keeping our eyes open, shifting left and right. I looked over to my right, and Bolo looked like he was succumbing to the music. His eyes were glazed over, and he had dropped his arms down and dropped the hammer he had been holding. As I watched, he began to drift and stagger ever so slightly in the direction of the well. I dropped the shovel and, bracing myself against the swirling winds, tried to get to Bolo.

His eyes looked blank. I was sure he no longer knew what was happening around him, or to him. I tried to shout to Gooby, who was on the other side of Bolo, but he was looking the other way and couldn't hear me. All manner of branches, leaves, and debris was flying through the air. Bolo was oblivious to them all as he stumbled closer and closer to the well. I had to swat away branch after branch just to keep moving forward. I reached out to him, hoping that our hands could connect, and I could pull him away before he fell into the murky depths. He looked at me—or rather, he looked through me. His eyes were empty, and he made no effort to raise his hand to meet mine. The music kept droning on and on in my head. It was dizzying. A large branch hit the side of my head and staggered me. I fell to my knees. With one last herculean effort, I lifted myself up and lunged towards Bolo. As I fell forward, I was able to grasp his Van Halen concert t-shirt. With all my weight, I fell forward, pulling him and his shirt downward. He stumbled, fell toward the fort, and landed awkwardly against it.

I pulled myself up and as I did so, another evergreen bough, partially broken from the tree but still attached by a strand of bark, swung down, hitting me full in the face. Like an Olympic diver standing on the end of the board with his back to the pool, I teetered, windmilling my arms like crazy, desperately trying to regain my balance. In a split second, there was a gust of wind, and I knew all was lost.

In that split second before I plunged beneath the cold, dank water of the well, it wasn't my life that flashed before my eyes, but one specific memory—one memory that was burned into my brain and required no effort to recall at a moment's notice. Unlike me at the moment, the memory was never far from the surface. It was also responsible for the fact that I had avoided learning to swim for the first twelve years of my life.

From the time I was an infant, my family took an annual camping vacation. We went to the same campground in the upstate New York Adirondack Mountains every single year. Sometimes we even had the same campsite more than one year in a row. For my family, it was the highlight of the year. My dad came from a large family of nine kids. Every year my family, my grandparents, and several of my dad's brothers and sisters and their families would all convene on the campground for the same week or two. At times, it seemed as if the campground had been overrun by my cousins and me. As a kid, it was a dream come true. Days spent exploring the woods and getting rides in Uncle Harold's boat. At night, there was always a campfire and toasted marshmallows.

Of course, there was swimming as well. Every campsite had a little bit of lake access. It was a small lake—shallow and calm most days. It was perfect for kids to frolic and play games in. As a four year old, I had very rudimentary swimming skills from the few lessons I had at The Aquatic Club over the winter. In spite of my lack of experience, I wasn't at all afraid of the water or the lake. They were a part of our playground every summer. I couldn't really swim, but I could wade out up to my waist and splash around with everyone. One of my older cousins had been paddling around on an orange pool float. I wanted to try it so bad. For some reason, it just looked so cool to be lying on your stomach paddling as if on a surfboard.

When my cousin grew tired of it and came ashore to warm up by the fire, I grabbed the float and began to paddle myself around, not too far from everyone. I would watch the little minnows swimming in schools below me and follow them as I paddled. As one of the smallest fish in the sea, so to speak, the minnows would try to hide from larger predators. Being a large, orange thing floating on the surface and following them must have given the tiny fish the impression that I was some kind of giant mutant shark pursuing them. They darted and zigzagged their way into a forest of lily pads. I lost sight of them, as well as of the bottom of the lake. I wasn't any further off shore than I had been when I started pursuing the minnows. Little four-year-old Cooper didn't have a whole lot of endurance, and I had grown tired of paddling, so I decided I'd hop off the float and walk back to shore.

Obviously, you see coming what I did not that day. I was literally in over my head. I casually slipped of the float, expecting to feel my feet hit bottom, while I could still see the sun, but in a moment of indescribable terror for a small child, my feet never found bottom. Also, apparently at four, I was composed of mostly lead, because I sunk under the water like nobody's business. I couldn't swim, but I was great at sinking. I'm comfortable saying that I had mastered the skill.

My feet did eventually find the bottom, but I had a lungful of water, and I was hopelessly entangled in the lily pads. As I tried to push off the bottom, I remember the terror I felt, as I believed that the stems and roots of the lily pads that were wound around my legs were living and were trying to pull me down as I fought against them. Then, as if from the heavens, the canopy of vegetation that had closed on the surface above me parted and two hands reached in, pulling me back into the sunshine. As my cousin Tina carried me to shore, I coughed and sputtered to get the water out of my lungs.

Like most young kids, I was resilient and within minutes, was wrapped in a towel, warming myself by the fire. All appeared to be well, but somewhere deep within my psyche, the near drowning had permanently placed a chink in my armor. I still remember the feeling of those lily pad stems tangled around my legs. In my four-year-old memory of the event, they were alive, actively clutching at me, trying to pull me down to the bottom with them forever, as if they were tiny, slimy little arms belonging to some evil lake creature that wanted to devour me.

After that day, I avoided swimming in water over my head. I actually had avoided swimming. The guys had never noticed because those of us that had swimming pools had above-ground pools that were no more than four-and-a-half feet deep. I never had to learn to swim. Until now. Yup, now suddenly seemed like an ideal time to expand my skill set.

When my foot slipped off the edge of the well and I plunged into the dark, cold water, I immediately seemed to instinctively fall back on my long dormant skill of sinking like a rock. I wanted to call for help, but my mouth was full of disgusting, brown water. The light from above grew dimmer. Then, in a moment of clarity, I remembered where I was. The well.

I spread my legs and arms out to brace myself against the walls. My descent stopped. I used my toes and fingertips to propel myself upward a few inches at a time. I wanted to push hard and jump towards the surface but that just resulted in me slipping and backsliding.

My lungs burned. I was starting to feel dizzy, and that music was playing again. It was happy music. I started to feel relaxed as the song played in my head. It was telling me that everything would be all right. That's when I felt it. That's when the terror seized me.

My toes slipped a little down the well walls as I tried in vain to cling with my fingertips like some sort of aquatic Spider-Man. That's when I felt the slippery tendrils reach up from the deep to encircle my legs. First the right and then the left. The song was telling me they were embracing me. I don't know how the music told me these things without words but in my mind, I just wanted to believe the soothing rhythm of the notes.

Then, in a flash of memory, I recalled the lily pads and how they had tried to pull me down. I wasn't going to give in. I wasn't going to let them try to take me again. I began to thrash about violently in the narrow underwater space, trying to throw the cold, wet, pulling tendrils off my legs. Just as one broke free, I would feel another take its place. They seemed to be climbing up my body, wrapping themselves around me. I was afraid to let go of the walls with my hands for a second, lest I be pulled down into the cold darkness. I kicked and kicked. The more I fought, the more they seemed to entangle me.

I was running out of breath and was beginning to think it might be easier to stop resisting—to just allow the cold, dark water to fill me. I would just slowly drift away. *There would be no more struggle or fear if I just give in*, I thought. No, that doesn't feel right. I didn't think it. That thought, that feeling of despair, didn't come from me. It was projected into my mind.

There was a flash of illumination from above, and I looked down as I fought the little snake-like arms entwined around me. In a blur, I saw a face, a human face. There was someone down there and his arms ended in the long, slippery tentacles that were grasping at the lower half of my body.

I glanced upward at that flash of light, suddenly feeling strong hands grasping my wrists. I was violently pulled upward and in a jumbled moment of noise, brightness, and pain, I found myself on my hands and knees on the forest floor next to the well, coughing up some of the dankest water I had ever seen, or unfortunately, tasted. It burned coming up through my nose. I wasn't trying to cough or vomit, but it seemed that my body was going to violently expel the filthy water as hastily as it could, whether I liked it or not. When I stopped coughing and my eyes stopped watering, I looked around.

Cliff and Gooby were wet from the chest down and were sitting there just looking at me. Bolo was also sitting nearby and appeared to have regained his senses. The vortex of nature that had engulfed us earlier was nowhere to be seen. The woods looked as they had when we entered. The sun shined down in broken rays through the foliage, and the birds were back to chirping. I collapsed onto my back and said, "RR. Robert Ruttinger. Oh, and I could kill for a Creamsicle right now."

Chapter 22

I don't know what it was, but when I was under water, I had some sort of epiphany. Maybe the threat to my life galvanized my thinking, or maybe it was something I gained by some sort of osmosis when I had physical contact with that thing down there. *If* there really was anything down there grabbing for me. Who knows? A lot of things that were happening to me this summer were starting to seem very unreal. I wondered if maybe I was crazy and didn't know it yet.

When I landed on the ground after being pulled from the well, suddenly some pieces of the puzzle had fallen into place. Granted, they weren't all the pieces, but they were a start. I coughed again to clear my throat of a little more of the disgusting brown water that I had swallowed. Gasping, I tried to get a full breath of air into my lungs and my brain. I didn't like how my breathing still sounded, and felt—wet. The guys just sat there staring at me as I cleared my lungs.

Bolo obviously couldn't wait to find out why I had uttered his name after nearly drowning. "What? Why did you say my name? What did I do? It wasn't my fault you fell in," Bolo said.

I took a deep breath again and hesitated. "Ok," I said, "as long as you guys promise not to call me crazy, I'll tell you what I thought of." I looked around the circle at all of them as they looked at me. They looked at me as if I was crazy.

"Thought of?" Cliff said. "You were down there drowning, and you were thinking? Maybe you should have been thinking about swimming or something." That drew a few smirks from the guys, but my near drowning had been serious enough that nobody burst right out laughing. I had to admit, if only to myself, that was pretty funny. I wish I had said it.

"Funny, Cliff," I said with a wry smile. "Listen though, I think I'm on to something." I needed another deep breath. I hadn't quite got my wind back. "I don't know why we can't remember it, but something did happen to us when we went into that mausoleum. I know you guys can sense something is missing from our memory of that night. At least that's how it feels to me." They all nodded in agreement. I had their attention. "Robert Ruttinger and Amanda Arseneau.

Both double letters for their initials. It means something. When that… that thing had a hold of my legs, it was like it was reading my mind and I was reading his, its, whatever."

"Wait, wait, wait," Gooby interrupted. "What do you mean 'that thing'? What thing? What was down there?"

I explained my blurry memory of how I had seen Bolo being drawn towards the well and how I had fallen in when I was trying to pull him back. Then I mentioned the music, the song. For a moment, it was as if a light had gone on in their heads. The moment the spell or whatever it was had been broken, the music stopped and we all forgot it. They all agreed they heard it and that it caused some sort of feeling, some sort of pull in their mind. The song seemed to cast some kind of hypnotic spell upon us all at once. When the thing with the tentacles touched my skin, it triggered some type of telepathy and I could remember and understand. I hesitantly began to describe, as best I could, the person or creature I had seen at the bottom of the well. Mostly all that I recalled was a blurry, human-like face and the long, slippery tentacles that seemed to be everywhere around me down there. No one had seen it when they pulled me out.

I wondered if they all thought I was crazy. Now that I had been here conscious, breathing and thinking, it seemed like whatever I had remembered was starting to fade like a dream does shortly after you wake up. It wasn't a dream though. I wasn't crazy. *I know something is going on*, I thought to myself. *I have to convince them before they all forget that crazy tornado that just spun around us a few minutes ago.* That's when it struck me like a blow to the head. You know, when you hit your head hard and you see that flash of bright light for just a split second? That was the exact feeling.

"Ice cream!" I literally shouted. "It's the ice-cream song!" That's when the puzzle pieces fell into place for all of us. I could see it dawning on their faces after the realized what I was saying. The hypnotic little tune that kept mesmerizing us was the song that the ice-cream truck plays when it comes through our neighborhood. That song is like catnip for kids. The ice-cream man is like some sort of pied piper. "Now someone or something is using the song to, I don't know, lure, kidnap, and kill kids."

"So wait," Bolo interjected, "are you saying the ice-cream man is trying to kill me? What an idiot! All he'd need to do is give me a cone of cookies and cream, and I'd be a goner." We all chuckled a little at that. We had grown used to Bolo's attempts to normalize his diabetes by making jokes about it. I felt bad for thinking about him being different every time he pointed out his diabetes. I suppose I should be the last one to look at him differently, considering my inability to handle lactose. I can't have milk, and he can't have sugar. I guess it's not really that different, except if he has too much sugar, he could go into a coma and die. What happens to me if I have milk only makes me die of embarrassment. Of course, I didn't have to have shots a couple times each day either.

"No, you idiot! I did not say the ice-cream man is trying to kill you!" I said as I gave Bolo a shove. "What I'm saying is that someone or *something* is using that song to sort of hypnotize us, but I don't think he, or it, is trying to kidnap and kill just any kids."

"You know what it sounds like to me?" Gooby interrupted. "It sounds like we might be dealing with a Karabasan."

After we all rolled our eyes almost simultaneously, Cliff said, "Ok, Cliff Clavin, I'll bite, what is a Karabasan?"

"I'm glad you asked," Gooby replied with a smirk. "A Karabasan is an evil spirit, or goblin, in Turkish folklore. The creature is believed to have hypnotic powers that it uses to lure its' victims away from others. In old English, the translation of Karasaban is *maere*, or in modern linguistics, *mare,* which is what the word night*mare* is derived from. The Karabasan's victims are said to be found dead without a mark on their bodies. They are believed to die from suffocation. In ancient times, they believed that the Karasaban, or evil spirit, would lure children from their homes at night with its' hypnotic song and while they were paralyzed, much like sleep paralysis, it would suffocate them by sitting on their chests. It's either that or a vampire." He sat back, arms folded, with an insufferably smug look on his face. One day we would learn the phrase autistic savant, and apply it liberally to Gooby at times like these.

Chuck laughed out loud and said, "Yeah right, Goob. A vampire that lives underwater? Vampires don't swim!"

"Who says?" Gooby replied. "Who makes up the vampire rules? Old movies or stories? There's a reason that vampire stories have been around forever. Every fairy tale or myth starts with a grain of truth. If you're so sure vampires can't swim, maybe it's a Siren like in the Greek myth about Odysseus. The sirens lured men to their death with a song. A song. Sound familiar? And where did we just pull you out of? Water. Where were the Sirens in the Greek myth? They were on the rocks in the ocean, which is made of what?" Gooby was really getting his smug on now. Hopefully, we'd be able to mock him about his crazy theories after this was all over.

With as much sarcasm as he could muster, Bolo said, "Is it just me, or does everyone want to punch you in the face all the time?"

"Umm… well, ok, moving on," Cliff continued. "There's only been one kidnapping and killing. You said it was a serial killer before. Why do you think he's trying to kill Bolo?" Cliff asked, looking at me. "He hasn't kidnapped him yet, right?"

I thought for a moment, trying to plumb the depths of my mind. I knew something was in there. It was like an itch that I couldn't reach. I knew that the answer was playing hide and seek with my mind. It was there, I knew it. We all knew it. Again, I had that sense of reaching into murky darkness, feeling around, trying to find something that just kept slipping off my fingertips as I got close enough to grasp it. That feeling was enough to drive me crazy. Then I found it, or part of it. It was part of that dreamy memory that hadn't completely faded away yet.

"Bolo, I fell in the well when I pushed you away from it! Now I remember. You were sort of stumbling towards the well. You looked like you were out of it," I said. "It wasn't me that was supposed to fall in, it was you! The song was pulling you there."

"Yeah Coop, you saved his life," Chuck said sarcastically.

"You're a hero. You know what, Bolo? After you hit me in the nads with that pinecone, it would have served you right if you fell in the well. You might want to watch your back; I just might push you in next time," he said with a sly grin.

Bolo sat silently, not responding to Chucks chiding, as if he were lost in thought. "The cubbies," he said quietly, almost under his breath. We all just looked at him. "The cubbies," he said again. "Something about the cubbies.

Don't you guys remember the cubbies? Cliff, you were there. You too, Coop."

Cliff shook his head. "I have no idea what you're talking about. What cubbies?"

Bolo looked over at me with a plaintive look, "C'mon Cooper, you've got to remember. You were there."

Again, I had that slippery memory feeling, like I knew that what he was talking about was down there somewhere in the dark corners of my mind, as if my brain had tried to hide that memory away from my conscious recollection. I kept reaching into my mind. It was there. Then, suddenly from the darkness, I pulled out Bolo's red bandana. It had sprung to the front of my mind as if I had suddenly pried it loose.

"You and Amanda Arseneau both have double-letter initials. That seems like too much of a coincidence. Each of the cubbies had two of the same letter on them.

Something sounds very familiar about that. I'm going to have to ask my dad. I think I've heard of this before. He would know."

"Your dad would know? Know what?" Cliff asked skeptically.

I gave an exasperated sigh. This would be so much easier if we had a talking stick or something. "My dad watches the news," I said. "Like, obsessively. I think he has a crush on Dan Rather. Anyway, he watches the news. If there has ever been a serial killer in the last thirty years with an MO involving double letters, my dad would remember it." Yeah, that's right; I slipped MO in there. I had no idea what it meant, but I heard it on Miami Vice, and it sounded pretty damn cool when Crockett had said it. Hopefully, the guys wouldn't call me on it.

"Wait, I've got an idea!" I exclaimed. As exhausted as I was, I still quickly scrambled to my feet and headed in the direction of the southeast corner of the woods. I reached *The Sneaker Tree* ahead of everyone else and stood there, my eyes searching the tree. I didn't see it at first, but when I moved around to see the other side, there it was. As the others caught up and stood around me, I just pointed at it. It was a camouflage Converse high top nailed to the side of the tree. It was one of Bolo's sneakers—the one that had been missing from his foot when we rescued him from under the cemetery. I would bet it we looked hard enough, we would find one of Amanda Arseneau's sneakers up there too. This was where the killer hung his scalps. It was like his little shrine to the lives he had destroyed, or possibly, sadly, it was his trophy display. The thought sickened me. It turned my stomach to think that each of these sneakers that had mysteriously appeared here over the last six years or so, represented a life taken.

We looked around the woods. All seemed calm with only the sounds of breeze, birds, and crickets to observe what was about to happen. Then we did what no one had ever dared to do. No one had ever taken a sneaker off *The Sneaker Tree*. We didn't know why. It had always just seemed that the way the sneakers mysteriously appeared, gave it some sort of untouchable aura that would be bad to break by touching it.

Chuck sat on Cliff's shoulders, reached up, and, with a little effort, pulled Bolo's sneaker off the tree and handed it to him. "Hey, thanks guys," he said. "This was my favorite pair of sneakers." We decided very quickly that we should probably get out of the woods, just in case.

Chapter 23

Our next game was the first of the playoffs. The Mullane Motors Yankees were coming in as the number-one seed. We had lost just one game all season, and that was probably only because Cliff was gone on vacation with his family that week, and we just didn't have enough pitching.

Today, we weren't too concerned. We were playing the worst team in the league, and we had mercy'ed them last time we played. The "Mercy Rule" is that if one team is up by ten runs after four innings, they call off the rest of the game in the name of sportsmanship. I went four for four with six runs batted in last time. I was licking my chops at the thought of facing them again, and in the playoffs no less. I still didn't have my home run and was getting desperate and swinging a little too freely at the plate.

I felt a little like I was losing my mojo at the plate, so this morning, I had dug up the courage to go over to Scooter's house and ask his mom for something of Scooter's to wear in the game. I told her that I wanted to take a little piece of Scooter with me in the playoffs. I saw tears well up in her eyes at that. "Of course, dear, come in, come in. I think he would want you to have whatever you want. I want you to have it."

I stepped in the open door and as it closed behind me she just stood there looking at me for a moment. Then she startled me by taking a step closer and hugging me. "Thank you, Cooper. Thank you for remembering him. Follow me. You can help me find something in his room," she said, her voice faltering a bit.

We went down the hall and into his room. She opened the door, and it was just as I remembered it, only dustier and with no dirty laundry on the floor. The blue, Yankee Stadium outfield wall painted below a pinstriped top half of the room was still there. He even had one of those AstroTurf kind of rugs on the floor. I was so jealous. I wish my dad cared enough to paint my room like this. Then I bit my tongue, or I guess I bit my thoughts, when I remembered that Scooter was still dead, even if I had been seeing him and talking to him all summer. I thought to myself, *Do I dare tell his mom about seeing him? Would she want to know that he's alright? What would she do if I told her he is hanging around at the baseball field?*

This was awful. I know she didn't know what I was thinking, but if I told her that I saw and talked to the ghost of her son, she would probably freak out and ask me a million questions and then I'd never get out of there in time for the game. That settled it. I wasn't going to tell her.

She opened the closet to show me all of his Little League shirts from the past few years. They looked washed, pressed, and hung up as if it were a display in Cooperstown. On his dresser were his baseball and basketball trophies and one Pinewood Derby trophy from scouts. Over on his desk was the picture of him that had been on top of his coffin at the funeral and next to it, the glove. THE glove that I had been so jealous of when Scooter had been alive. The grey and black Nike model that looked like it had magic in it. I don't think I had ever seen a grounder get by Scooter when he had that glove on. I thought he'd been buried with it.

I didn't want it because it was an awesomely cool glove. I wanted it because it was Scooter's awesomely cool glove. If you've never played baseball, you wouldn't understand how attached we get to our gloves. They have to look and feel just right. After we get them broken in and soft, they feel like part of our hand when we slip them on.

I remember the day Scooter had gotten this particular glove brand new. He had worn it all day. He came over to my house wearing it. He wore it when we walked around the neighborhood. He had a ball he was constantly throwing into his glove to break it in. He even kept it on when we stopped to have lunch at my house. I'll never forget how funny he looked holding a peanut butter and jelly sandwich in his glove. He didn't mind getting peanut butter on it. He just rubbed it in like it was that glove-softening oil the pros use. It must have taken a month for the peanut butter smell to wear off. If there was one thing of Scooter's that would give me some mojo, it was that glove.

"Umm... Mrs. Grottanelli," I gulped as I said it. "Do you think I could borrow Scooter's glove?" I asked, pointing to it hesitantly.

She looked at me with those big, watery eyes and a wan, sad little smile. I was afraid she was going to hug me again. "Yes dear. Of course you can. He loved that glove, and I know he'd be happy to know that it was still somewhere catching ground balls." Then she did hug me again.

Geez, I thought to myself, *does everybody get this emotional when they get old?* I also swiped a batting glove from the desk on my way out. I didn't want any of Scooter's batting mojo because, honestly, he was a better fielder than he was a hitter, but I had lost one of mine and didn't want to play in the rain without them.

It was rainy today, but as long as it didn't get too bad and there wasn't lightning, we were going to play the game. I arrived with Scooter's glove tucked under my arm, just in time to line up for some warm-up throws. As usual lately, Chuck and Andrea were throwing to each other. Gooby nodded in their direction, and I just nodded my head to indicate that I had seen them. My first instinct was to tease him. My second was to be jealous. I just stuck with the second and tried to focus on the game.

As was our new tradition before taking the field, and especially because it was the playoffs, we all put our hands in, one on top of the other, and Cliff led us in the chant "We're young, we're tough, and we're good looking!" It was still worth a laugh every time.

In the first inning, Cliff's dad changed up the batting order because this was the playoffs—no more equal-opportunity lineup. We wanted to win and our batting order and fielding positions showed that. Cliff led off the game with a single up the middle. I was second in the order and, on the first pitch to me, which was a strike, Cliff stole second base. He was in scoring position. The expectation was that I'd put the ball in play, either a hit or a deep fly ball that would score Cliff, and we would be up 1-0 in the blink of an eye. It was good strategy as far as Little League went. Unfortunately, I struck out. I struck out bad too, embarrassingly just flailing away at the ball as it went past me in what appeared to be slow motion.

I went back to the dugout, head down and shoulders slumped. That kid didn't have the stuff to strike me out. *What had happened up there?* I threw my bat and batting gloves down, grabbed Scooter's glove, and sat down on the bench. "Dude, what are you doing with my glove?" It was

Scooter. He was sitting right next to me, practically on Gooby's lap. "No, seriously, if you have my glove, I can't play the field." I tried to look straight ahead as if nothing crazy was going on, while Scooter explained some hokey ghost mumbo jumbo about why he couldn't have his ghost glove if I had the real one.

Whatever, I thought to myself. I was still feeling mad about the strikeout. "I guess you'll just have to be a ghost runner," I said aloud as I jogged out to my second-base position to start the bottom of the inning. Again, I was a complete ass to a ghost. *The kid is dead—why did I have to act like a jerk to him*, I thought to myself. Now I felt even worse. This was just not my day.

I was still lost in thought when, out of the blue, I heard "Ting!" Andrea's first pitch was a hit and it was a hot grounder right at me. It hit the lip where the infield grass met the dirt of the base path and took a wicked hop. There was no thought, just reaction. I didn't even see the ball. It was like my mind saw the bounce and threw my glove up there without conscious thought. I fielded it cleanly, jogged two steps towards first, and tossed it to Gooby. As the spectators on our side applauded, I gave a wave of my glove as I returned to the ready position for the second batter. *Damn*, I thought, *now I know why Scooter loves this glove so much.* Then I caught myself, *Loved. He loved this glove*, I reminded myself. I still felt like a complete heel as I saw Scooter sitting in the dugout.

In the third inning, we were up 2-1 when I got my second at bat. The same pitcher was still out there. He threw so slow that I wondered how the ball stayed airborne long enough to cover the forty-five feet and six inches between the mound and home plate. It was absolutely excruciating to stand there in the batter's box and not swing for that long after he let go of the ball. I didn't strike out this time, but I might as well have. I hit a pop up to the catcher. The catcher! How embarrassing is that? I'll tell you how embarrassing it is. I had to endure catcalls from Goob, Chuck, and Bolo as I walked back to the dugout.

In the bottom of the fourth, we were still clinging to a one-run lead. Bolo was in to pitch for us and had walked the first two batters. That was definitely not good. The first pitch that Bolo attempted to unleash to their clean-up hitter was rocketed back, right at him. I had a momentary flashback of Scooter getting hit, but fortunately, Bolo got a glove up to defend himself and the ball ricocheted off it and straight up into the air. The runners took off, and so did I. After three full speed steps towards the mound, I was on the infield grass. I dove horizontally in the air with my arm outstretched. The ball dropped into my glove just inches above the ground. I quickly rose to my knees, threw over to Gooby at first, and he in turn threw to second. Both runners were doubled off! It was a triple play! Maybe the first in league history and it was all because of Scooter's magic glove.

It was the top of the sixth and final inning the next time I came to bat. It was likely my last at bat of the game, as we were still desperately clinging to that one-run lead against the worst team in the league. Cliff was on third and Scooter was on second, not that it mattered. What did matter was that there were two outs, so I'd have to hit a fair ball to score him and give us a little breathing room. I finally felt like I was getting my timing down against their slow pitching. I'd fouled off the last two, so I knew I was getting close. Here comes the next pitch. I watched and watched. It looked good all the way. No movement. It was heading for the center of the plate. I loaded my weight back and as it arrived, I turned on it and lashed it hard to left field. It looked like it was going to go out! I started sprinting towards first as Cliff jogged home. As I rounded first, I had a clear view of the left fielder backing all the way up to the wall. Then that was when I think my mind went a little haywire. On the other side of the fence, just a few feet from the left fielder, I saw a man casually leaning on the fence, arms folded and a smile on his face, as if he were having a grand time watching the game. When I realized who it was, I stumbled and fell right in the dirt as my ball was caught. *Genzler!* It was *Genzler*! What was he doing here watching our game? *That is freaking weird*, I thought to myself. As I lay in the dirt, I pounded my fist on the ground in frustration before I got up and dusted myself off.

When I got back to the dugout, I pointed him out to the guys as we prepared to go out for the bottom of the inning. Bolo seemed particularly creeped out by the fact that *Genzler* was there watching us, and that was unfortunate, because he still had to pitch.

Fortunately though, I ended the game with another spectacular catch. We won by a score of 2-1, but I felt lousy about my hitting. It was my first 0-fer of the whole season! As we picked up our stuff in the dugout, I noticed that *Genzler* was gone from the left-field fence. I sure hoped he didn't try to grab one of us on the way home.

"That's a damn shame," the gravelly, old voice said from behind me. It was Mr. Gregersen, the elementary school janitor. Apparently, he also was groundskeeper for the Little League field. He dragged a big, gray garbage can behind him as he picked up the candy wrappers and sports drink bottles left behind from the day's games. I looked at him quizzically. "It's a shame your last hit didn't go out. That was a beautiful swing," he said. "At least you played a great game in the field. Man, your glove was on fire today."

I smiled. "Thanks, Mr. Gregersen. I didn't know you watched the games." Everyone else had already left the dugout and were either talking as they walked towards the trail home, or headed for the parking lot. As I looked past Mr. Gregersen, I noticed Chuck and Andrea walking away together and, for a moment, they linked pinkies when they thought no one was looking.

"Oh, yeah. I watch'em all," Mr. Gregersen said. "I used to play a little too. I was a shortstop when I was your age. I grew up down south though, in Florida. We could play games all year-round down there. I played with a kid named Vince DiMaggio. Vinnie was ok, but you should have seen his little brother. Now there was a ballplayer. He was two years younger than we were, but he was so good he played up a level and was still as good as we were. You remind me of him a bit."

Unfortunately, I wasn't really paying attention enough to really appreciate the compliment he had just given me. I really wanted to catch up to my friends and maybe tease Chuck and Andrea a bit. "Yeah, thanks Mr. Gregersen. See ya' later," I shouted as I jogged away, trying to hook my bat bag over my shoulder clumsily as I ran. I wanted to catch up to the guys to see what they thought of *Genzler* hanging around the outfield fence. Somewhere in the back of my head, a pleasant little song began to play. It just barely tickled my consciousness, not enough to grab my attention though, as I focused on catching up to my friends.

Chapter 24

The rain from earlier in the day had let up and that evening, as usual during the summer, Bolo, Gooby, Cliff, Chuck, and I ended up walking around the neighborhood after spending a couple hours swimming and hanging out at Gooby's house. Although it was evening, at this point in the summer, the sun was staying up late and consequently, we were allowed to stay out a bit later as well. We were kind of walking ourselves dry, still in swimsuits with towels over our shoulders. Some of us were barefoot and some had opted for sandals. Our neighborhood was off a main road but, in general, wasn't very heavily trafficked, so with our burgeoning, almost adolescent egos, we walked in a group right in the middle of the street as if we owned the place.

At first, we focused our creative energies on teasing Chuck about Andrea. After a few minutes, we ran out of innuendos that we really didn't understand, and some that probably didn't make any sense, and we finally got down to what it seemed like we had been avoiding all day. Bolo broached the subject first. "So, what do you guys think we should do about *Genzler*? Should we call the cops?"

Cliff snorted somewhat derisively. "Call the cops and tell them what? That we think our neighbor is a serial killer who lives in a well in the woods and plays the ice-cream truck song?" He did have a point. That story did sound more than a little far-fetched. Bolo still looked a little miffed at Cliff's disparaging dismissal of his idea. I didn't blame him. I was all in favor of telling the cops everything we knew and had seen, except for Scooter. It was one thing if the cops thought we were all just stupid kids, but it was a whole other ball of crazy if I told everyone that I was seeing and hearing someone that no one else was.

We were stuck. We didn't have any hard evidence to prove anything. All we had was some ridiculously imaginative stories that sounded like they came from a horror flick. "Hey guys, wait a minute. I think we might have something we can go on. I asked my dad about the double-letter initials thing. He told me that about ten or fifteen years ago, upstate, there had been a series of killings involving children with double-letter initials. He said that the murders were never solved. They just stopped. He also said I could go look it up on the microfiche at the town library. Yeah, like that's gonna happen."

"No, wait, your dad may be on to something," Cliff exclaimed.

"Yeah, right about now he's probably on to his sixth beer," I grumbled. It was the most I had ever admitted to the guys, but no one said anything. The silence hung there awkwardly for just a beat longer than I was comfortable with. I had hoped to just slip it into the conversation and let it go.

Cliff continued, "No, seriously. If this serial killer likes kids with double initials, we can go through the yearbook and see if there is anyone else he might go after next, and if worse comes to worse, we can use Bolo as bait!" Cliff looked smugly at us, as if he had just revealed the secret to the creation of the universe. Bolo's mouth was agape.

"What? Wait. No!" Bolo sputtered. "Why does it have to be me?" His eyes kind of spun crazily in their sockets as he looked back and forth between us.

"Well," Cliff said, "you heard Coop. It's the double initials that this killer gets off on. I really wish I could do it, but it's the initials. You got'em, and he wants'em!" In spite of Bolo's current anxiety attack, we all laughed a bit. I suppose it was easier for us to laugh because we weren't the ones who were the proposed bait for a serial killer. "Don't worry about it, Bolo. We'll be nearby, and we'll make sure we do it where we can catch him. He won't know what hit him," Cliff concluded.

After a lengthy argument and with our assurances that we wouldn't let anything happen to him, Bolo reluctantly agreed. We talked out our plan as we walked a couple more laps of the neighborhood before darkness fell. It was settled; we would set our trap and capture the killer tomorrow night.

Chapter 25

That night, as usual, there was tension in the house. My parents were busy being miserable and angry in separate rooms, so I decided I'd sneak out and go talk to Scooter. Talking to him had been a Godsend this summer. As usual, I slipped out my back window. I didn't even worry about my parents. They had become so self-absorbed lately that I sometimes wondered if they even remembered that I lived there. Just to be careful, because there was a serial killer around, I stayed on the street until I got to the corner, and took the left onto the little extension that led to the quick trail to the back of the field. I was relieved not to run into Bolo tonight.

Scooter and I played a little ghost baseball before settling into our usual walk around the inner border of the field. He, of course, asked how things were at home. "I feel like they're so wrapped up in being mad at each other that they wish I wasn't around," I said.

"Now, you know that isn't true," Scooter replied. "They may not care about each other too much, but they care about you. I know what you're going through. My parents almost split up about two years ago. They got through things. Maybe yours will and maybe they won't, but you know what? It has absolutely nothing to do with you."

I laughed a little. I knew he was right. "What are you laughing about?" Scooter asked.

"You," I answered. "You turn into a ghost and suddenly you're all mature and wise? I can't believe I'm getting life advice from the kid who had to go to summer school for math last year." I shook my head and chuckled a bit more. We kept walking and talking, and spent a little while just sitting in the dugout.

While we sat, I noticed an odd thing. A firefly landed on Scooter's shoulder. He didn't seem to notice.

When its little illuminated tail glowed, the light seemed to fill Scooter a little bit, at least his shoulder anyway. That's not what piqued my interest though. I would have expected that. What surprised me what that the firefly landed *on* him. It didn't fall through him. We were talking about our families, so I just filed that little fact away to ask him about later.

"So," I started, "umm, have you figured out why you're still stuck here at the baseball field? I mean, it's not like I'm complaining 'cuz I like coming here to talk to you and all, but it's gotta be getting pretty boring for you." I don't know if it was my imagination, but at that moment, the night got even more still and quiet than it had been. Scooter kept talking. Apparently, helping me had made him think he had free license to let loose with his beliefs on virtually everything. Then again, he wasn't doing too much talking at all lately, so I let him go on and on. The stillness of the night had me unsettled though, so I kept one ear open for Scooter's monologue and the other keenly attuned to the rest of our surroundings. Not even the crickets dared break the silence.

This wasn't good. I didn't feel right. It wasn't cold, but I was getting the chills. The darkness in the direction of the cemetery and the woods was just too dark, too complete in its inky blackness. Scooter rambled on and on. Man, he was on a roll. I heard mention about Blair and Jo from some show he was rambling on about. I wasn't paying attention anymore. I was watching the darkness. When I had first looked over, it appeared that the cemetery and woods had disappeared into blackness. Now when I looked in that direction again, the outfield fence seemed to be lost. I shushed Scooter and pointed towards the outfield. Maybe it was all just the nervous little mind of a twelve-year-old kid, but I didn't think so. The silence and the darkness were to complete. That's when Scooter whispered to me, "Run!" He sounded afraid.

There was no thought on my part. I did what he said and ran. I ran to the light of my street on the other side of the trail and the trees, but didn't stop there though. I ran down the street as fast as my feet would carry me. I tripped and fell once, scraping my hands, but I got up and kept running. I tore into my backyard and, in one leap, landed upon the top of the picnic table. I threw the screen up, clambered into my room, and fell on the bed. I didn't care about my parents hearing. Slamming the window shut, I locked it. Somewhere in the back of my mind, I heard a pleasant little song playing. I was so tense and filled with adrenalin that I couldn't imagine I would sleep at all. I kept the light on in my room and wondered to myself, *Was that the last thing Amanda Arseneau saw—the darkness coming to get her?*

I awoke the next morning, surprised and panicked for a moment because I hadn't wanted to fall asleep. It appeared, however, that I had survived the night. I thought about Gooby's vampire theory and the myth about vampires not being able to enter a home unless they were invited in. *Nah,* I thought to myself, *Gooby can't be right about this. I won't let him. It's just too stupid to be true.* Besides, what twelve-year-old wants to believe that a vampire might be stalking them?

What I did remember from last night specifically was Scooter's words of wisdom, and I felt a little bit better. Scooter was right and as my dad always said, this too shall pass.

Chapter 26

The twenty-four hours between hatching our plan and launching our plan seemed interminable. We spent the next day talking about it constantly, no matter what we were doing. I had even watched a few Miami Vice reruns last night just to get ready.

We also spent quite a bit of time scouting out the location. We had chosen the baseball field. It was wide open and we could see someone coming from any direction. It also had fences, further limiting the serial killers escape routes. We were pretty cocky. We had thought of everything. The weather forecast was a little sketchy, but we hoped for the best because right now it was warm and sunny. Hopefully, it would be dry tonight and without fog. I was glad for that. I hated the fog. It just creeped me out ever since I had seen that movie *The Fog* a few years ago. I definitely did not want to be out in the fog trying to capture a serial killer. I was also perfectly happy to let Bolo be the bait. Bolo, however, still felt differently.

Bolo couldn't understand why the rest of us just didn't understand his reluctance. The rest of us were insulted that Bolo didn't trust us with his life. Four twelve-year-olds against a serial killer, what could possibly go wrong? "C'mon Bolo, lighten up," Chuck said encouragingly. "Just make sure you check your blood sugar before you come out tonight, and everything will be fine. I'll even bring juice boxes and crackers!"

"Oh great," Bolo moaned. "You can save my life by squirting berry blast right in his eye."

We planned to meet in front of Cliffs' house after we all had dinner. That was when life threw me a curveball—at dinner. Usually, at twelve, life's' catastrophic curveballs are pretty benign. They're most often things like your family going on vacation during Little League playoffs or your favorite show getting cancelled, except if Miami Vice got cancelled. That would be really bad. Crockett and Tubbs were my role models. The real curveballs in life don't tell you they're coming. They just broadside you when you're not looking on any random Thursday afternoon.

Like every other Thursday, for as long as I could remember, we had spaghetti for dinner. I'm not sure why we did this. We weren't even Italian. We were Irish though, so thank God Mom didn't make us eat corned beef and cabbage every Thursday. Or any other day for that matter, really. I did love the smell of the sauce cooking when I got home.

The meal started like every other 'family' meal, with silence until it became awkward. That was my family—champions of the awkward silence. We had it down to an art form. It was definitely tougher since my sister went to college. My sister used to bail me out sometimes by chattering away about her boyfriend drama. Now it was just them and me. It was like a dinner table game of chicken. My usual tactic was to just dig in and pretend my mouth was too full to talk. I might nod my head or give a grunt now and then to show I was listening. You could feel the silence getting heavier by the moment…

until someone cracked under the pressure and blurted out whatever they could think of.

This time it was my mom. She asked when my next game was and commented that they might try to make it. I tried to look like I believed this, but I think they knew I didn't. They didn't even know it was the championship tomorrow! It was like we were living entirely separate lives. I was just about to chastise them for not knowing when my mom spoke up.

She said they were getting separated. I knew what that meant—divorce. At first, I wasn't sure what to feel or think. They both just stared at me for a minute, waiting for my reaction. I felt like an animal at the zoo as they watched me. They looked completely dumfounded, and on the edge of their seat. I had never had this kind of attention from my parents. I pretended to chew my food really thoroughly while I pondered this new development. When I could chew no more, I swallowed what was left and took a swig of my lemonade. Yeah, I know lemonade with spaghetti sounds weird, but since I was lactose intolerant, I didn't have much choice. It was either that or water.

"Ok, well, I'm gonna get going. I promised the guys I'd meet'em right after dinner," I said as I stood up, pushed in my chair, and walked out of the room. I didn't even look back. Trotting to my room, I grabbed my bat and glove, since we were allegedly going to be playing ball tonight before sleeping over at Gooby's house.

As I was leaving my room, I noticed Bolo's lucky bandana on the floor from the other night. I grabbed and shoved it in my pocket thinking, *He'll definitely want this for good luck tonight.* As I headed out the front door, my parents were still in the dining room, apparently not willing or interested in confronting me to find out my reaction to their big announcement.

To me, it wasn't big news. I didn't have a big reaction in me. I could have told you about three years ago they'd be getting a divorce. Either they didn't know it until recently, or they were actually still trying to fix things these last few, painfully tense years. As far as life's curveballs coming at you, this was an easy one to hit out of the park because I had been waiting for it for a long time. I was relieved.

It was only about 6:15 pm when I ran out the door and headed for Bolo's house. It looked like some ominous clouds were gathering on the horizon. Hopefully, any rain might hold off until after we were done. I also hoped that it wasn't a bad omen. Bolo was already nervous enough. I didn't want him to have any easy excuses to back out of our well-planned fiasco. I had just learned the word *fiasco* and was fond of using it whenever I could, to the point that the guys were starting to mock me for it. I hoped for Bolo's sake that tonight wouldn't be a fiasco.

I decided that I would cut through the backyards to get there. If I took the street, I'd have to go right by *Genzler's* house. First and foremost, I didn't want his creepy stare-down, and secondly, if he was *The Poetry Killer*, I didn't want him to see all of us gathering together and acting all awesomely covert and whatnot.

What I didn't take into consideration until it was too late was the fact that if I passed *Genzler's* house on the street, I would also be passing it as I went through the backyards. In my mind, I guess I just thought that everyone's house was set up like mine with the living room in front. I imagined that even *Genzler* and his dad would sit in front of the TV and watch the evening news in the front of their house. I realized my error when I found myself behind his house. I stayed as far back from the house as I could, skirting the tree line in the back, hoping that if he looked out, I would blend in with the foliage. I wasn't dressed in camouflage or anything. I just hoped that if I

stopped moving when he looked, he might not see me.
Kind of like when you're a little kid in bed at night, and
you're sure there's a monster in your closet but somehow
you just know that if you don't move, he won't see you.
Apparently, I had a lot to learn about being sneaky. *I might
as well just try to play dead,* I thought to myself just before
I was hit in the head with a blunt object and dragged into
the trees.

Chapter 27

I awoke, or at least I think I did, with excruciating
pain in my shoulders. Don't get me wrong, my head
throbbed like nobody's business from the blow. I might
even be concussed, but it was the pain in my shoulders that
roused me to consciousness. Oh my God, it was awful.
What the hell? I thought. Then as my brain became a little
more focused, I realized that I was hanging by my wrists,

which were tied to a metal grate above me. There didn't seem to be any floor beneath me, and I was blindfolded.

In very short order, I also realized that my mouth was duct taped too. Or was it *duck* tape? *Damn it,* I thought. *I'm going to lose my mustache hairs when that comes off.* Yeah, I had two mustache hairs. I was pretty proud of them. Thank God he didn't duct tape me anywhere else. Come to think of it, it probably wouldn't matter.

In taking stock of my situation, I began to think I was kind of screwed. Let's see... kidnapped by a killer? Check. Unable to see, speak, or use my hands? Oh yeah, I am all over that. Unbearable itch on the bottom of my left foot that I can't reach? Got that covered too. *I am the man,* I thought to myself. Ok, no I didn't. What I did think was, *Oh my God! I'm going to die!* I was screaming that in my head over and over, until I was distracted by the itch on the bottom of my foot. It was driving me insane. I almost wished *Genzler* would kill me now, just to make the itching stop. That's when I realized that my itchy left foot was bare, and the sneaker that had been on it was probably nailed to a tree in the woods.

What would Sonny Crockett do in this situation? There has to be a way out of this, I thought to myself. Then it hit me. I could feel my feet, and they weren't tied up. If I could tolerate the pain in my shoulders, I could swing my feet about. At first, I tentatively moved them a little side to side and discovered that I was in a narrow space. They easily hit what felt like a cement or stone wall on both sides of me. I braced them against the walls and briefly lifted myself to take some of the strain off my aching shoulders. I hadn't realized it until I was able to support myself by my feet, but my breathing had been quite shallow. I relaxed a little bit and took a few deep breaths to clear my head and give me a little energy.

Crap, if I want to swing my feet forward or back to see what's there, I'm going to have to let myself down and hang from my arms again. I took a few more deep breaths and considered whether I was ready to inflict that pain on my shoulders again, when my left foot slipped a little. I used my toes to push myself up a little further so that I could grab the metal grate with my hands and was no longer hanging by my wrists.

I took a deep breath and let my toes slide slowly down the walls, until I was hanging by my hands. The pain was back but I gritted my teeth, biting into the tape, still not sure what to call it, but not too worried about it at this point. I'd have to look it up before I told the guys this part of the story. Otherwise, it would turn into a whole fiasco that I'd never hear the end of.

I began to sway my hips to get my feet swinging. Forward and back, little by little, I began to swing. As each twinge of pain shot through my shoulders, I thought, *I sure hope they don't need me to pitch tomorrow.* Then I felt my feet hit a hard, cement wall behind me. I swung forward without hitting anything. As I swung back, I angled my feet so that

I'd be able to push off the wall for maximum swing. The Air Jordan on my right foot and the heel of my bare left foot hit the wall. With all my strength, I pushed off and swung forward so fast I was afraid one of my arms was going to pop out of the socket. A shot of pain went through me. As I extended my legs, my feet hit a wooden surface, and I swung back with a little more knowledge than I had a minute ago.

Ok, I thought to myself, *cement may not break or even make a sound when I hit it, but wood just might.* I chuckled a little. I was twelve. We always chuckled when someone said *wood*. Thinking of one of our stupid jokes when I was possibly about to be killed made me feel a little better and made me think about the guys. I was supposed to meet them. *I wonder if they know I'm missing? Are they looking for me?* As these worries ran through my head, I remembered why I had chuckled about wood in the first place. There was a wooden surface in front of me. If I could kick it hard enough, it might break or someone might hear me.

I had braced myself against the walls with my feet again to take the pressure off my shoulders. As I stood there, taking a deep breath, I could feel myself sweating in spite of the cool, damp air around me. *I must be underground,* I thought. Then a drop of sweat ran down my nose, over my upper lip, and into my mouth. The hot, salty taste reminded me of when I had given mouth to mouth and CPR to Scooter that day. I swallowed to keep down a little bit of nausea. As much as I loved Scooter, I hoped today wouldn't be the day I'd join him on that baseball field. *Damn it, I wish he were here to help me.*

Well, it's now or never, I thought to myself as I sort of leapt off the walls to get my swing started. The pain in my shoulders was excruciating. I swung my legs, forward and back, forward and back, trying to build enough momentum to hit the wall behind me and push off. With the blindfold on, I had no idea how close I was. After the third swing, I felt my toes touch the wall behind me. Then, suddenly I heard it. The ice-cream truck song. I knew I only had moments before he, or it, was here. Or before I lost conscious control of my body. On the swing back, I anticipated the wall, planted my feet, and pushed off as hard as I could, immediately straightening my legs in front of me. My shoulders screamed in pain. The volume of the ice-cream truck song was almost deafening within my head. It was maddening. I mentally braced myself for impact with the wall.

When I expected my feet to hit the wooden wall, I heard a noise, like a door creaking open, and I felt a whoosh of fresh air. My feet hit nothing, and I swung back and forth until my body came to rest. I braced myself with my feet against the walls. The music droned on and the pain in my shoulders seemed to fade away. "You lied to me," he said. "This isn't your bandana."

I couldn't see him. The voice sounded both familiar and unfamiliar at the same time. "You tricked me," he said. Then I knew it was Mr. Gregersen. It kind of sounded like him, but just a little off. There was a malevolent rumble, an undertone to the voice, that wasn't usually there. It chilled me to my bones as I hung there helpless. "You don't have the initials I want, Cooper Scott," he went on, speaking slowly. I could hear the disgust in his voice as if it was dripping off his tongue. "But you're going to die just the same."

Holy crap, I thought to myself. *It's true. Psychopaths do rattle off a crazy monologue before they kill you. Or maybe Mr. Gregersen has just watched too*

many movies. It's funny, the things that go through your
head before you're going to die. Apparently, that whole
'life flashing before your eyes' thing is a myth. I should
have asked Scooter, I thought.

"OOF!" At least that's what it sounded like. Then I
heard bodies hitting the ground and a lot of scuffling and
several more "oofs". It was maddening not being able to
see what was going on. Then I heard "FUCK!" At least I
knew Cliff was here. As I hung there, I heard punches,
kicks, and what sounded like head butts. Or at least I
imagined I did. I assumed that The Golden Boys were just
kicking some serial killer ass. I mean really, how could it
go any other way? Then I heard a sort of dead, muffled
crack combined with a hollow, metallic sound.

Of course, now you're expecting some crazy
reversal of circumstances where there's silence, and then
Mr. Gregersen speaks again to chill me to the bones, and
confirms that he has defeated my friends and now intends

to kill me. Much to my pessimistic surprise, I heard the voice of Gooby say, "Hey Cooper, you didn't think I knew how to use a bat. Ha!"

Then I heard Chuck, "Hey Cooper, are you alright?"

I breathed a sigh of relief. "Yeah, I'm ok, but I'm not sure I can pitch tomorrow."

Then I heard laughter. "Pitch?" Cliff squealed. "You know I'm getting the start. We won't even need you. What the hell are you doing in there anyway?"

"Oh, you know," I replied, "just hanging around."

What I regarded as hilarious at the time was met with groans all around. In short order, they had rescued me from the crypt. As soon I the blindfold was taken off me, I looked around at the three of them, and at the ground around them, and said, "Where did Gregersen go?" They all immediately had a panicked look on their faces as they whipped their heads back and forth, surveying the ground around them in the fading light of dusk.

"Shit. We lost him. Fuck. We shoulda' tied him up," Cliff said. The rumble of thunder overhead seemed to agree with him. The wind was picking up loose leaves and beginning to toss them about.

"Wait," Chuck exclaimed. "Where's Bolo? He was here with us during the fight."

We all looked around and called his name. I even tried shouting "Marco" to see if I'd get our trademark reply of "Bolo!" It was to no avail. Gregersen, or whatever he was, was gone, and he had exactly what he wanted—Bolo and his damn double initials. He had used me as the bait. We had to find him and fast, or Bolo wouldn't survive the night.

As the sun went down, the wind picked up and those ominous rumbling clouds finally arrived from the west. We could see the strobe effect of the heat lightning and could feel a little static in the air. After losing one of our own, we decided it was definitely better to stay together. The cemetery appeared to be deserted, but with the limited light and the wind, it was hard to see and hear everything, especially someone, or something, who didn't want to be heard. We could see that the baseball field appeared empty, so we decided to try to search the woods.

"I know where to start," I said confidently. I'm not sure why I knew this, but I just had a feeling in my bones that I had to follow. I hoped to God that it wasn't a false feeling that Gregersen had planted there to lure me, or us, to our doom.

"Let's walk slowly in a circle," Cliff suggested, "so we have someone looking in every direction." We all nodded our heads in agreement. I led the way, with Cliff and Goob on the sides, and Chuck walking backwards watching behind us. That was sort of his lot in life at that point, regardless of the situation, but he put up with it.

"This way," I said. I started slowly toward the side of the cemetery where the opening in the fence was. We were all in front of the entrance to his underground lair when the guys rescued me. The baseball field was clear. There was nowhere else to escape to. He had to be in the woods. It was the only place left to hide.

I was feeling pretty cool leading our little expedition. It was just past dusk so it wasn't completely dark yet, but it was getting there, and it certainly would be darker in the woods.

I wasn't too worried about finding our way in the woods. We knew those trails like the back of our hands. *Why do they always say that? Who spends a lot of time looking at the back of their hands?*

The wind was still picking up, and the treetops were leaning in unison with it. The dark clouds seemed as if they were stalking and threatening us, warning us to get inside. They had that angry, malevolent look that storm clouds have when they look like they're bearing down on you. Then I felt it. I felt the air change. It was suddenly cooler and had that familiar smell to it. I kept looking up at the sky, as if that was where the threat was coming from. I had momentarily forgotten we were trying to rescue our friend Bolo who had been taken by a serial killer, or vampire if Gooby were to be believed.

That momentary distraction was all it took. I banged my shin painfully on a short, stubby grave marker and fell forward into the dirt. It happened so fast that Gooby, Chuck, and Cliff all tripped over the marker as well, and we ended up all in a heap, cursing. Because they had fallen on top of me, I was last to get up. As I pushed myself off the ground, I glanced at the small tombstone that had been our downfall. *Gregersen.* At least, that's what I thought it said. The light was mostly gone and after the fall, I didn't want to embarrass myself more with the guys by freaking out about something that was at best just a bad coincidence. That's when the heavens opened up with rain and all hell broke loose.

Chapter 28

It started slowly at first with those fat, round rain drops that almost look like big, wet marbles dropping so slowly that you can see them falling and can almost catch them in your hand. I could hear the splat of each dollop of water until their assault upon the Earth gradually began to gain speed. We felt like we were under attack with the rat-a-tat-tat of the rain getting faster and louder. It wasn't sensible or rational, but being twelve, we still had a bit of little kid brain in us, and we panicked when there was a flash of lightning, followed immediately by a deafening clap of thunder.

We just ran for the hole in the fence and the cover of the woods. We forgot about Bolo and Gregersen for a minute, and fled Friedhof Cemetery as if our lives depended upon gaining safe haven in the woods. Instead of running away from danger, we were running straight into it. Based on what happened in the woods before, I couldn't be entirely certain that Gregersen hadn't conjured up the storm to drive us into a trap of some sort. When we got to the hole in the fence, there was a little bit of pushing and shoving as we jostled each other, but got through without injuries or fights.

We headed straight for the trail that we knew would take us into the woods and to our fort. As soon as we entered the woods, we were thrown into darkness. I don't know if it was our fear or our imagination, but the darkness seemed unnatural, as if it was darker than it should be. We paused for a couple seconds, catching our breath and falling into our circle formation just like before. In spite of our run-for-our-lives mentality, we had gotten soaked to the skin. We had to shout above the hiss of rain hitting the canopy of leaves one hundred feet above us. Again, it felt crazy, as if nature was being whipped into a frenzy to oppose us.

My shoulders were rising and falling with each short, ragged breath I took. The others looked as shaken as I felt. At that moment, I felt a tingle in the air, and I got goose bumps all over me. There was a peculiar smell in the air. Then, a blinding flash of white light and a boom I heard and felt to my core. Without even realizing it, I was on my back on the ground, as were my friends around me.

As we got back up, I looked up into a flickering orange glow and an intense heat coming from above us. I still hadn't regained my bearings yet when I realized that the source of the flames appeared to be getting closer.

"Look out!" I screamed, pointing upward.

Most of a large tree that was engulfed in flames was falling in slow motion towards us, its progress downward slowed mercifully by other trees. I didn't need to look. I knew. I knew what tree the lightning had hit. It was *The Sneaker Tree.*

I felt a shove as I fell to the ground. Chuck and I rolled and scrambled away on our hands and knees. I hoped that Gooby and Cliff were as fortunate. The tree had come crashing down where our group had been standing, and split us apart. It might have killed us had we frozen in place when it fell. *Wait a minute,* I thought. *I did freeze. Someone pushed me!* It couldn't have been Chuck. He was at least ten feet away when we were picking ourselves up off the ground.

I couldn't see where Cliff and Gooby were through the flames. Suddenly, I realized that I couldn't hear. The thunderclap that had occurred literally on top of us must have temporarily deafened me, and probably Gooby, Cliff, and Chuck as well. I felt a tug on my arm, and there was not Chuck, but Scooter.

It looked as if Scooter was trying to talk to me, but I couldn't hear him. He gestured at Chuck, who was waving for me to follow him as he ran along the length of the fallen inferno that was what remained of *The Sneaker Tree*, giving it a wide enough berth to protect himself. I understood what he was doing. If we went far enough to get around the end of the tree, we could get to the other side and find Gooby and Cliff.

In spite of the rain that was filtering down through the branches and leaves above us, the fire continued to rage and spread. The dry pine needles on the forest floor seemed to catch every spark that leapt from the flames and, in turn, gave birth to another little incendiary demon. The forest around us was suddenly alive with little, orange dervishes.

They seemed to be everywhere with their tiny fingers of flame reaching for my feet and my legs as I ran. It was a miracle that neither of us fell. We ran, leaping over flames and tree stumps as if we were in one of those commercials where O.J. Simpson is running through the airport.

As I ran, I could see the sneakers burning on the tree, which was now mostly engulfed in flames. It seemed to be an omen of some kind. I hoped it was a good one. For a moment, a thought flitted through my mind. *Shit! I'm never getting my other Jordan back now.*

The lightning continued to tear through the sky like a jagged knife, briefly adding illumination to the surreal scene we were in the midst of. Thunder rolled and boomed so near I could feel it. The crackling of burning wood and the hiss from rain falling through the trees added to my disorientation. If we didn't get out of there soon, smoke inhalation would be one more problem to add to our list. This definitely wasn't going like we planned.

We rounded the end of the fallen tree to see our fort not too far from the spreading inferno. I wondered if Bolo, or Gooby and Cliff, could be in there. There was only one way to find out. I caught up to Chuck when he paused. Tugging at his arm, I pointed to the fort. My hearing wasn't fully back yet, but I did have a buzzing in my head. It reminded me of how I felt after Bolo's brother took us to that Ramones concert up in New Haven back in May. Buzzing was better than nothing, so I guess that was an improvement. In spite of the buzzing, I still heard the familiar, happy singsong melody of the ice-cream truck pulling at my soul, but I think the buzzing in my head dampened it. It didn't seem like the undeniable gravitational pull I had experienced when we had been underneath the crypt.

Chuck must have also lost his hearing because he pointed at his ear, nodded at me, and then pointed towards the fort. We started towards the fort, leaping the well as we ran. I didn't see Gooby and Cliff anywhere, but that must be where they went. I can't imagine them not checking there first.

Chuck and I reached the fort at the same time and tore the rickety door open. There on the floor was Bolo. He appeared dead. We moved inside and I took his wrist to check for a pulse or see if he was breathing. BAM! I nearly jumped out of my skin. The door had slammed shut behind us, or was slammed by someone. I was startled and about to panic when I realized that it was just our fort, not a crypt or a bank vault. We had put this thing together so shoddily that I knew we could just kick down a wall if we needed to.

Crouching down near Bolo, I put my ear down in front of his mouth. A worthless move I realized, when I remembered that I couldn't hear anything. As I looked at his chest, I could see it rising and falling. He was alive. Chuck and I breathed a sigh of relief, but only for a moment. We could hear the flames crackling outside the back wall. Chuck gave the door a push, only to find it wouldn't open. I felt the back wall and quickly pulled my hand back. It was hot. Too hot. It wouldn't hold back the flames much longer.

My hearing was starting to come back, but I tried to mime to Chuck that we needed to get going, that we were going to have to bust our way out of there. He shook his head in puzzlement. Ugh, what a terrible time to find out that I was a lousy mime. I shouted. Just because I couldn't hear, didn't mean he couldn't. "Chuck! Break down the wall! We have to get Bolo out of here! Kick it!"

This was the perfect instruction for Chuck. Over the past two years, he had become a rabid fan of some cartoon involving anthropomorphic turtles who knew karate and battled evil. He was always telling us about it and practicing his karate kicks, as if they might invite him to be one someday. We did think he was a mutant—that much he was right about. He always swore that he was going to be a spy or secret agent when he grew up, so I figured now was a good time for him to start. I mimed a kicking motion toward the door and pointed to him. He nodded and exhaled slowly as he assumed his stance.

In a smooth, fluid motion, he loaded his weight on his back leg, reared back, and coiled his front leg in the air in front of him. I saw him push forward and unleash one hell of a kick against the door, which popped open with the sound of splintering wood. We picked up Bolo, with me lifting his upper body by hooking my hands under his arms, and Chuck grabbing his legs. It wasn't the most graceful method of transport, but Bolo was unconscious, so he wasn't complaining.

The air wasn't much fresher or cooler once we got outside the fort. The flames battled against the rain for purchase in the forest. As more and more brush and trees caught fire, I looked around for just a moment, feeling a little sadness at the prospect of our woods being gone. That thought was fleeting as I realized that we'd better keep moving if we didn't want to be gone as well. Then I heard, "Coop! Chuck! Over here!"

Thank God, I thought, as I heard Cliff's shout. We dodged burning branches as we struggled to carry the unconscious Bolo across the uneven forest floor. Each step was treacherous as we moved slowly forward, trying to avoid tripping over tree roots and ending up in a heap on the ground. Again.

I could see Cliff waving us over, and then I froze. In front of Cliff and Goob was Gregersen, or whatever Gregersen had become. I don't know if it was real or a reflection, but he appeared to have fire in his eyes. He stood defiantly, staring us all down. He had a body in one of our baseball uniforms in one arm, and a jagged-edged knife in the other. It was a big knife. Probably the biggest I had ever seen. It looked like it could tear through a car door. He slashed it crazily in the air in front of him. No words came from his mouth, just a terrible, inhuman growl, which seemed to emanate from somewhere deep inside him.

We carefully set Bolo down in what looked like a relatively safe spot, away from anything burning. Chuck and I turned, moving slowly towards where Cliff and Gooby seemed to have him sort of cornered near a big tree. He didn't seem to be backing up though. We spread out so that we almost encircled him. It was crazy. I was terrified and hyperventilating, which was not good. I was taking in too much smoke, so I had to slow my breathing. I pulled my t-shirt neck up over my mouth to act as a filter.

What the hell did we think we were doing? A bunch of kids advancing on a cold-blooded killer with a serious knife? I had a very bad feeling about this.

That's when Chuck suddenly screamed, "Put her down!" I looked closer and saw the blond hair hanging down from the head of the unconscious figure in Gregersen's arm. It was Andrea.

Where the hell did she come from? How did he get her? I grabbed Chuck's arm and held him back from charging at Gregersen. Gooby and Cliff had frozen on the other side of him.

He continued to wave that big knife around, as if daring us to come after him. He seemed to realize that we had slowed our advance when we saw who he had in his arm. I couldn't tell if she was dead or alive. There was no obvious blood anywhere on her, but in the darkened forest with the flickering light of the flames as our only illumination, it was hard to really see details. I couldn't tell if her chest was rising and falling with her breathing either.

Then I blinked. I blinked because I thought I saw something. Something was moving behind Gregersen! I wasn't sure. I didn't want to hope. It couldn't possibly be true. I watched and waited as we all engaged in this bizarre little dance that would most likely end with death. I saw it again. A flash so quick as to be almost imperceptible. Almost just a shadow. At first, I wasn't sure if it was just smoke or perhaps my over-taxed senses seeing what I wanted to see. Then I saw the smoke pass around a shape. It was what I thought it was. Scooter!

It was impossible to believe, but it appeared that Scooter was about to try to pull off maybe the oldest of schoolyard pranks—right here, right now. I thought he was crazy, but what choice did we have? We didn't know how much longer Bolo would last if his blood sugar was low, and we had no idea if Andrea was even alive or maybe just barely clinging to life in his arms. If we didn't get out of the burning woods soon, none of us would have much of a chance to survive.

As I watched, the wraith-like form of Scooter got down on his hands and knees directly behind Gregersen.

Do we wait and hope for the best? I wondered. Then, as Gregersen stood his ground, I made up my mind. I quickly took a lunging step forward. As I did this, I scooped up a club-like piece of branch from the ground and brandished it towards Gregersen. He slashed wildly at it, connecting twice. He tried to step towards me, but I poked the branch straight at him, causing him to step back. He was tantalizingly close to falling over Scooter. But would he fall over Scooter? Or would he just walk through him?

For only fraction of a second, Chuck and I made eye contact and in his eyes, I saw all I needed to see. He knew. He saw Scooter. I lunged forward with the stick again, and Gregersen slashed at me, slicing into my forearm, but as he did, the back of his legs hit Scooter. He let out an animalistic howl as I saw the surprise in his eyes as he fell backwards. When he hit the ground, Andrea rolled from his arm, and Chuck bolted into the fray to grab her and pull her unconscious body to safety. Well, relative safety anyway.

With cat-like reflexes, Gregersen was back on his feet and wildly cutting through the air all around him with a knife that was now tinged with my crimson blood. Goob and Cliff had taken a step forward, but backed off just as quickly. The flames were closing in on us, and flaming branches began to fall to the forest floor around us. *What now?* I thought. We had made our big play, and Gregersen was still alive and ticking. He seemed to sense that he had the upper hand and began moving towards us, still wielding the knife like the lunatic he obviously was. We had him outnumbered, but he had the weapon and seemed completely oblivious to the burning forest around us.

"Beetlejuice! Beetlejuice! Beetlejuice!" Chuck shouted. For a split second, all of us turned our heads to look at Chuck. Gregersen too. Chuck just shrugged his shoulders with a sheepish look on his face as if to say, *What? It was worth a try.*

Then I heard it. First a *whoosh* then I heard another bizarre sound. Someone was hooting and hollering. We all looked up in the direction of the noise. Even Gregersen paused to look with us. Like some sort of angel or demon, a dark figure came flying towards us through the flames and smoke on our zip line, and he, or it, was the one doing the hooting and hollering. "Woooo Hooooo Hooooo! Ha Ha Ha!

I was pretty sure it wasn't Batman, because I had never heard him hoot or holler in a movie. *Oh great, another maniac,* I thought. *What the hell goes on in our neighborhood at night?* I hoped that this lunatic would at least be on our side and not just fight Gregersen to see who gets to eat us first.

All four of us dropped to ground in fear. Gregersen stood his ground, waving the big knife crazily in front of him as if this were the final standoff in some sort of movie. I could only hope it was good versus evil, and that triumph would be on the side of good. As the dark figure flew through the air straight for Gregersen, I saw a flash of silver. He was swinging something himself. As he got closer and I could see his weapon more clearly, I couldn't believe my eyes.

His weapon had a logo. I recognized it. It was my baseball bat. For an instant, the figure was lit clearly, as he flew past a burning branch. In that brief moment, I realized that it was *Genzler!* He was on our zip line, hanging by one arm and swinging my bat like a polo mallet in the other hand. And he was hooting and hollering like he was having the grandest time in the world flying down that line. "See, Chuck," I said, "that is how you zip line one-handed."

Chuck took the time to flip me off without taking his eyes off the maniacal, flying *Genzler*.

The four of us were frozen as the incredible scene unfolded in front of our eyes. Helpless to do anything but watch, completely dumbfounded, I forgot everything around me. The forest ceased to burn. My freshly gashed arm was forgotten, and I just watched. I'd swear *Genzler* was smiling as he approached the end of the line that was tied to the tree over Gregersen's head.

As he flew downhill on the line, his speed built and the speed of his right arm windmilling around with my bat at the end of it like some crazy scythe. Gregersen took one final swipe with the knife and missed Genzler's leg. As Gregersen's last, desperate swing followed through, the bat, seemingly acting as some sort of magical scythe, flew through the air in a perfect swing. The sweet spot on the fat part of the barrel connected perfectly with Gregersen's head and for a split second, my eyes registered the momentary look of surprise on his face as his head came clean off and flew through the air.

We all watched as it arced through the air, the eyes now blank and the mouth frozen in one last, defiant snarl. It seemed impossible, but I watched as that perfect rainbow of an arc ended with Gregersen's head plunging into the cold, murky waters of the well. At first, there was just a normal splash, as if someone had thrown a head-sized rock in. Then all seemed to fall silent for a moment until we heard at first a gurgling, then a kind of bubbling, coming from the well.

We approached it slowly and carefully, just barely leaning in towards it to see the surface of the water, which looked like it was starting to boil. It was churning from within. From down deep, there seemed to be a disturbance in the well. I started to hear (feel?) that ice-cream truck song again. We had encircled the well, watching—unable to tear ourselves away. For a minute, maybe more, we seemed to have forgotten our friends, who might be on the verge of death already. We forgot about the woods burning around us, and the flames growing closer. Our fort was ablaze nearby, and it barely registered with us.

Afraid to get closer, I was fearful of slipping on the edge and falling into the terrifying, murky darkness that had almost taken my life once already. I was fearful of that song starting in my head again and pulling me in. Then it happened.

You know those wind-up Jack-in-the box toys? You know how when someone is winding one up and that little song is playing, and you can't help but lean in closer in anticipation? That's what we were doing. I don't know if it was edge-of-your-seat anticipation or that damn song again, but we all seemed mesmerized by the churning water. Then a glow started to slowly build from within. I was terrified of that glow, but I couldn't pull myself away. I wanted to run but I was rooted to the spot. No one was speaking as the gurgle, boil, and churn built to a rumble and the luminescence seemed to be growing, rising, and getting closer to the top—closer to where we were all leaning over to get a better look. Leaning? Or were we being pulled?

Then the world seemed to explode in front of me. The water in the well shot straight up in a blood-red, luminescent, glowing geyser as wide as the well. It had to be at least thirty-feet high. We were showered with water. The singsong ice-cream song had turned into a tortured scream. We all fell back as if a concussive blast had knocked us over.

I lay on my ass, propped up on my elbows, looking up. At the peak of the shaft of water that somehow was suspended for what seemed like several seconds, there appeared to be a head, mouth open, emanating that hideous wail of pain that had replaced the ice-cream song in our heads. It wasn't Gregersen's head. It was as if the top of the geyser of water had taken on a semi-human shape and was crying out in agony. Then, as quickly as the tower of water had burst forth, it stopped, dropping straight back down into the well.

As it did, I felt a splash of water on my leg. I didn't worry because I was already soaked to the skin. Suddenly, I felt something pulling my leg. It wasn't a splash of water on my leg. From within the well, one of those slippery, slimy tentacles had reached out, grasped my leg, and was dragging me toward the well, which now seemed to be collapsing in upon itself like the house at the end of *Poltergeist.* "Guys!" I shouted.

My shout broke the spell and they all looked at me. The other guys seemed frozen, dumbfounded. Realizing what was happening, *Genzler* picked up the baseball bat, which was now stained with Gregersen's blood, and held it over his head like an axe. He stood over me, and I was afraid of what he was going to do. The bat started to rush downward, and I turned away and covered my head with my arms. *THUNK*! I heard the impact as the bat came down upon the arm of seaweed that was dragging me toward the edge of the well. Its grip loosened slightly, but it still had a hold of my leg, and I felt my toes slip over the edge.

I was on my stomach, grasping and digging into the ground, trying to find anything with resistance to hold onto, to slow my descent. I kicked at the green vine wrapped around my leg. *Genzler* wielded the bat again. I was afraid he was going to hit the thing on my leg when, suddenly, I felt hands grasp my arms on both sides and pull. The guys had me. At first, we were all being dragged. The ground around the well started to give, as it seemed to be being sucked into the earth. I could see them trying to find a way to brace their feet, but the forest floor was slippery with pine needles. "Pull harder! I can't get a good shot at it," *Genzler* shouted.

If I get out of this, I thought, *I'm going to have to starting thinking of Genzler's name without that tone in my head.* It was strange that I thought that right then, but I was right. All this time, years and years, we had all assumed Genzler was crazy, just based on rumors and stories. He had never really done anything wrong other than to stare at us. *We'll have to ask him about that.*

Suddenly, I felt my right arm stop. There was resistance. Chuck's foot had found a foothold against a root. Cliff moved around to join Chuck in bracing his foot and holding my right arm. Blood flowed from the gash Gregersen had made when he slashed me with the knife. Gooby anchored my left arm as best he could by being dead weight. "One, two, three!" Cliff shouted.

They heaved backwards, and I moved with them, although the vine thing still had a grip on my leg. I saw the root Chuck was braced against snap, and we started to slide back. Gooby and Chuck fell forward. Cliff's legs were scrambling wildly, trying to find some sort of foothold...

The ground around the well was giving way. We were all going in this time.

Whoosh! Genzler brought the bat down like an axe again on the seaweed arm that had my leg. I saw the logo gleam in the light of the flames as it whizzed by my vision. This time, the tentacle snapped and the guys all fell backwards, pulling me with them. We watched as the severed tentacle slipped back into the well, which almost seemed to have its own gravitational pull, as it collapsed inward on itself, pulling dirt and a few close bushes and saplings into its mouth.

God, I hope that's not a mouth or we're in trouble, I thought. Then, as suddenly as it started, it stopped. The well was gone. It had entirely closed. There was only a patch of a fresh earth where it had been. We stared at it for a moment before we were startled out of our stupor by the sound of our burning fort falling down nearby.

"C'mon. We should get out of here before the fireman show up," Genzler said. We picked up our two unconscious friends and carefully made our way to the entrance to the woods and out into the night. The sound of sirens was growing near. They would come into the woods from the road on the far side. We knew this from the time a couple years ago when a kid from down the street had accidently started a much smaller fire in the woods.

Chapter 29

We had made our way out of the burning forest and to a clear, flat spot in the field a safe distance away. Genzler had carried Bolo and set him down carefully. He pulled a juice pouch out of his jean-jacket pocket, punctured the skin with the tiny straw, and put it to Bolo's lips. He was still unconscious, so Genzler gave the pouch a squeeze. He repeated this a few times until the pouch was half-empty.

"If he doesn't wake up in a few minutes," Genzler explained, "we'll have to get him some help."

Chuck, of course, had insisted on carrying Andrea out and was attending to her as she regained consciousness. She was a little woozy and disoriented, but none the worse for wear. All she could remember was a trance-like feeling of following the music to the cemetery.

"So, umm... Genzler, how did you know where we were? Why did you save us?" I said.

"I know. I knew. I knew what was going on when that girl was found dead," he replied.

"Why didn't you say anything to the cops?" Gooby asked.

Genzler shook his head. "I knew what was going on, but I didn't know who. I knew because it happened to me."

Cliff looked up. "What? What happened to you?"

Genzler sighed. "My name is Greg. Greg Genzler. Double initials."

It took a moment for the light to go on, but then it hit all of us. Greg Genzler. GG. The double initials. "It happened to you? You were kidnapped?" I asked incredulously

"Yes, when I was sixteen," he replied. "I know what the stories are. I know everyone thinks I joined the military and came back crazy a couple years later. I didn't join the military. I was kidnapped, held hostage, and that thing fed off me for years. It was before I lived here. My dad moved us here from California after I came back. He thought he was getting me away from whatever happened and giving me a fresh start."

"That thing?" I said. "What is—was—that thing?"

"As close as I can figure, it's some sort of vampire…" Greg said.

"Boo Ya!" Gooby shouted. He shot his arms straight up in the field goal signal to celebrate. "Yes! I told you guys. I told you. I was right. Ha Ha!" he crowed.

"Wait, wait, wait," Chuck interrupted. "So it kind of lives underground and it *feeds* on people? That sounds like a C.H.U.D. to me."

"Shut up, you idiots," Cliff said. "Let him talk. So you said it fed off you? What is it? What does it do?"

Genzler, Greg, looked hesitant to go on. He sighed heavily and looked around our little group. He took a moment to check Bolo's pulse and shook his head affirmatively, as if to indicate that he was doing ok.

"When I was a teenager, I started to hear things. To hear music that no one else could. I'd run outside, looking for the ice-cream man, because I'd swear I heard his truck coming. That's when everyone started to call me crazy."

"We never thought that," I blurted out.

Greg chuckled a little bit. "Yeah, you did. I saw the way you guys looked at me when you walked by my house. It's ok. Everyone thought it. After a while, I realized that I was the only one who heard these things. So one night I followed the music and sometime later, I woke up, chained somewhere in some kind of underground dungeon. He kept me alive and kept feeding off me for years."

"What do you mean, *feeding* off you?" Cliff asked.

"I'm not sure," Greg replied. "I'd hear the music. He'd get closer, approaching me, and then I'd wake up hours or days later, I don't know, with a killer headache and feeling drained. Exhausted."

"Yeah, that's how I felt." We all jumped. It was Bolo. He was still on his back but up, leaning on his elbows. Greg handed him the juice box.

"I didn't know the alphabet thing until I had escaped, and a couple years later after I moved here. I heard of kids disappearing and turning up dead up near Rochester and Buffalo, and they all had the double initials, like I do. Like you do." He nodded at Bolo. "Then, a few months ago, shortly before that girl turned up in Friedhof Cemetery, I heard the ice-cream man again. That's what I think of him as."

"Well, if you knew he was at it again," I asked, "why didn't you just tell the cops to investigate Gregersen?"

"That's the thing," Greg replied. "He isn't always the same. I think he, or it, can change shapes or possess people. And it lives off of people, drawing something from them. It uses the music to lure kids. That's how I found you guys in the cemetery that time, and tonight. I still hear it."

Gooby looked smug as hell. Who could blame him? Finally, one of his crazy theories had panned out. *He's never going to let us forget this,* I thought. It didn't matter. He was still Gooby. Then again, maybe he was still Gooby, but with a little more confidence. I think we were all changed by our ordeal. I think if you're a twelve-year-old kid and you defeat a demonic serial killer together, you have a little tougher skin than you had the day before.

Chuck sat nearby, with his arm around Andrea. We watched as our woods burned. The firefighters were too late to save much of them. What we didn't know then was that it wouldn't have mattered if they had been able to save the woods. The land had already been bought, and was scheduled to be leveled within the next year to make room for another neighborhood.

Then Cliff stuck his hand out into the middle of the circle we had formed when we sat down. "C'mon everybody. Hands in. You too, Greg."

Greg Genzler looked a little confused but followed suit as we all stacked our hands on top of each other's. "Ok, on three, everyone. You know what to do," Cliff instructed. "One, two, three!"

In unison, we all said it. "We're young, we're tough, and we're good looking!"

On the walk back to our neighborhood, we were mostly quiet. Each of us was probably contemplating what our story would be to our parents if we got caught coming home. I felt a cold, metal tap on my left shoulder. "Here," Greg said, holding my bat out to me. "It's a good bat. A very good bat, I think. You'll need this tomorrow."

"Thanks," I replied, taking my bat from him. *Tomorrow?* I had forgotten about tomorrow. The championship!

Chapter 30

I had taken some gauze out of the bathroom medicine cabinet when I got home last night and bandaged my arm. It probably needed stitches, but I didn't want to have to explain it to my folks, so I just wrapped it and hoped for the best. That cut, and that night, would leave a scar I'd remember for the rest of my life. My leg also had what appeared to be a burn where the tentacle had grabbed me. My shoulders were sore as hell. I was a mess, but my parents didn't notice or give a shit enough to notice. I knew I wasn't supposed to, but I grabbed a couple of Tylenol from the medicine cabinet.

My shoulders ached in protest as I slipped on a long-sleeved baseball shirt under my jersey to cover the bandage on my forearm. I collected my glove, my bat, and my cleats. Pausing for a moment, I noticed a dark reddish-brown spot on the logo. The bat was already red and black, but the spot was a little different red, and was right on the silver part of the logo. Right on the sweet spot. The tiny smudge of something was no bigger than the end of a thumbtack, but wouldn't rub off, even when I licked the end of my thumb and scrubbed it. *Ah well*, I thought, *it doesn't matter. I'll get a new bat next year anyway.*

I left my room, heading for the front door, when I was stopped in my tracks by my father's voice. He sat in his recliner, looking over the top edge of the newspaper. He peered at me through his reading glasses. I could just see the top of his eyes and the hair that was beginning to gray at his temples. It occurred to me that my dad was getting older, and that maybe I was too.

"Were you boys out in the woods last night?" He looked at me with one skeptical eyebrow raised. That was an inherited trait I possessed as well, and would pass down to my own son, Nathan, many years from now.

"The woods? No. We were down at Bolo's, playing Ping-Pong. I won all three games. Why?" I was convinced that I was a brilliant liar, much like my hero Sonny Crockett was when he went undercover with the drug dealers.

"The woods burned down last night. Almost completely. I was afraid you and your friends might have had something to do with it. I know you go out there quite a bit," he said, never for a moment letting up on the skeptical look he was giving me. *His eyebrow must be exhausted,* I thought to myself.

"We did go out to watch when we heard the sirens, but that was it," I replied.

"Where are you going now? Do you have a baseball game?" he asked. "I thought that was done."

"Nope. Last game today," I answered as I headed out the door.

Chapter 31

Gooby and I met in the street and walked to the field together. Chuck, Cliff, and Andrea were already there. There was no sign of Bolo. Immediately alarmed, I caught up to Cliff, who told me that Bolo's dad had called him this morning, saying that Bolo was having some problems with his blood-sugar level getting stabilized and would have to miss today's game. I was relieved to know that Bolo was still alive, but disappointed that he couldn't be there for the championship.

Although it was the championship game, all the talk amongst the players on both teams and the parents on the sidelines was about last night's fire in the woods. We could see what was left of the woods next to the cemetery, out past left field. It wasn't pretty. There was a lot of speculation about the cause of the fire. All of us kept our mouths shut and let the parents blame the older kids.

As we warmed up, taking some throws on the infield, I noticed Greg Genzler standing by the bleachers on the third-base side. Our side. He gave me a wave and a smile. I waved back and nodded.

It seemed strange to me that everyone was so focused on the woods burning and had no idea that we may have defeated, at the least, a serial killer, and possibly something even more evil. Looking back, it's hard to sort out reality from the wild imaginations of a bunch of kids playing in the woods. Whatever. I know what's real, and I'm reminded of it every time I see that scar on my forearm.

I'd love to tell you that we won the championship game on my walk-off home run in the bottom of the last inning, and that I was carried off the field on my teammate's shoulders, but that isn't what happened. Cliff, Gooby, Chuck, Andrea, and I were exhausted and sore from last night's adventure, and we played like it. We lost badly. We tried to be inspired and to play for Bolo, but physically, we just didn't have it in us. There was one interesting thing that did happen though.

In the sixth inning, I came up to bat for what I knew would be the final at bat of my Little League career. Next year, I would be moving up to school ball, and maybe a travel team playing on the big fields. We were down 6-0. There were already two outs, and I could see the other team laughing and starting to celebrate a little in their dugout. That always made me mad. It was disrespectful. It was as if they expected us to just to take our three outs and get off the field. Of course, it was ok when we did it, but I didn't have the insight to see it from any other point of view.

I hated being the one up with two outs in the last inning. There's nothing worse than being the out that ends the game. I was oh for two on that day. I was going to have to get a hit to avoid the ignominy of ending our season. My team was quiet as I approached the plate. They were expecting the end was imminent, and I could hear a few of them picking up bats and balls from the dugout floor.

I dug my cleats in the dirt. As I pushed my sleeves up, I noticed crimson red seeping through the bandage on my forearm. I looked to the pitcher and nodded as if to say I was ready. As he went into his wind up, I could see straight into the outfield behind him. What I saw made me forget to swing at the first pitch. "Steee-rike one!" the umpire bellowed. Jerk. I hated when umpires got all flamboyant with their strike calls.

Just shut up and call the game, I thought to myself. I shook my head, dug in, and looked again. What I saw made me smile.

It was Scooter, standing by the fence in left center. He was wearing his glove. The magic glove that seemed to catch everything. He waved it to me as if saying, *Hit it here—I dare you*. I nodded to him as the pitcher blew another strike past me. It was weird that Scooter was playing in the field. He had played with us and for us all season. Now he was opposing us? Two balls in the dirt followed. I was focused. Locked in. I wanted to hit it to Scooter. I wasn't sure why, but it felt like it meant something that he was there.

The next pitch was my pitch. I knew it when it left the pitcher's hand. It was coming in on a line, high and inside, but not so far inside that it wouldn't still catch the top corner of the strike zone. I swung fast, hard, and smooth, and it felt perfect. It felt like I had gotten all of it with the sweet spot of the bat. It was a rocket. The real fielder and Scooter were both running towards the left-field fence. Scooter got there and backed up against the wall. So did the real outfielder.

I tossed my bat aside and started to run to first. This was it. It was either an out or a home run. As I was running, I was trying to watch the ball's flight. As I rounded first, heading for second, I saw both Scooter and the real fielder leap at the fence. The real fielder leaped higher that I thought he could. I was so afraid he was stealing my last shot at the home run I had been chasing all season. Scooter, however, leaped a little higher, and I could see his ghostly magic glove extended just above the real fielder's.

If Scooter didn't keep it in the field of play, it was going to clear the fence. I actually stopped running between first and second to just watch at the ball hit the palm of Scooter's outstretched glove. As it did, it stuck there, pulling Scooter with it over the fence and into Friedhof Cemetery. As the ball hit the ground in front of a tombstone and bounced into it, I saw Scooter disappear.

"Run, Cooper! You've got to touch home," Cliff's dad shouted to me. He was laughing a little bit. I resumed jogging and as I rounded third, I saw my teammates gather in a circle around home plate. I arrived to pats on the back and head and as I dramatically stepped on home plate, making my first home run official, I stuck my hand out. Each teammate knew what to do.

"We're young, we're tough, and we're good looking!" we shouted as we threw our hands in the air and jogged back to the dugout. The other team looked at us like we were crazy.

As we sat in the dugout and watched the last out, Cliff handed me my bat, which I had tossed aside earlier. I looked at it to see if I could see where the ball had made contact. I could see it all right, and I wasn't surprised. Right where the red spot was from last night was two things—a ball mark and a crack. The bat was done, but that was ok. It had done its job.

Even though we lost, I walked home with a smile on my face. Not because of my home run, although that was pretty cool, but because Scooter was where he needed to be, a serial killer was no longer preying on children, Greg Genzler had gone from freak to friend, and through it all, I still had the best friends in the world.

Chapter 32

Piling the pillows and dirty laundry under my blanket, I quietly slid the window screen up. I slipped out as I had so many other times that summer. Cutting through the tree line, I took the path to the field. The lights were off, but I still took the walk from the dugout to home plate. I stood there for a moment, breathing in the cool night air and listening to the crickets chirp. I looked at the whole field and in my mind's eye, I watched the flight of my home-run ball. This time in my imagination, I only saw Scooter leaping to make the catch. It saddened me a little knowing that the Scooter I saw was only in my imagination.

I started to run the bases but when I got to second base, I changed my mind. I left the base path and walked straight towards the spot at the outfield fence where my ball had cleared it. Hopping the fence, the cut in my right forearm complained mightily. I hoped that it would heal without needing stitches, and without my parents knowing about it.

As soon as my feet hit the dewy wet grass on the other side, I didn't hesitate. The cemetery was no longer a fearful place for me. I walked straight over to where I saw Scooter disappear. There it was. My home-run ball was sitting on the grass in front of Nathan "Scooter" Grottanelli's tombstone. I looked at it for a moment before I bent over to pick it up. I gave the ball a little toss and caught it in my hand. "How about I trade you for it, buddy?" I said aloud. I took off my Yankees cap and placed it perfectly on the grass in front of Scooter's tombstone. Shoving the home-run ball in my pocket, I walked home.

It was never the same after that summer. We had lost Scooter, and then we lost two more of our group, although not nearly as tragically. We lost touch with Andrea when her parents sent her to Catholic school. That wasn't because of Chuck, but he was heartbroken just the same. Bolo's dad and brother took jobs as roughnecks on an oil rig in the gulf. They took Bolo and moved to

Louisiana just before school started. Gooby, Chuck, Cliff, and I didn't know what the future would bring, but one thing we did know was that after that summer, we would forever think of ourselves as *The Golden Boys.*

Other books by Phil Taylor:

White Picket Prisons – When *The Golden Boys* return to their neighborhood as adults what long hidden secrets will they discover?

Fifty Shades of Phil – The fifty best humor essays from the first eight years of his hilarious blog, **The Phil Factor.**

Also, look for his short story *Blog Stalker* in the ***Stalkers*** anthology to be published by editor Cynthia Shepp in November 2013.

About the Author

Phil Taylor is a father of three, husband to one, and life-long smart ass to many. He has been well trained by his two dogs and a cat and is a loyal servant to them all. Phil plays a mean game of Ping-Pong and claims to make the best grilled cheese sandwiches in the world, bar none. He has a Master's degree in Psychology and spent many years working in the field of mental health before realizing that stringing words together might be a little bit more fun. His two fiction novels, *White Picket Prisons* and *The Sneaker Tree*, are dedicated to his life-long friends that may or may not be very similar to *The Golden Boys*.

You can follow more of Phil's work by looking him up on the interwebs at:

www.thephilfactor.com

Made in the USA
Charleston, SC
23 December 2013